VENGEANCE ABOVE ALL

ANYTHING TO GET EVEN

ALEX J. FISCHER

For my Family and Friends

1

    —————

"Be careful with him now, boys," Richard said to the group of three surrounding the van. "If I see him so much as ding his shoulder, I'm holding all three of you personally responsible."

"We got it, President," the one in the middle said. He hooked Irving's arm over his neck. "You two get his other side."

The other two complied, and the three finally cleared the vehicle. Lucien hopped out of the passenger door. He sauntered over to Richard and stood by his side, watching the small group try to get moving. "How're the negotiations going with the Outback Boys?"

Richard's eyes never left the group as he crossed his arms. "It's going well. All we need to do is nail down the final numbers, and we're set."

"You'd better hurry," Lucien said. "There's no telling when our friends south of the border will pay us a visit."

"These kinds of things can't be rushed. You know that as well as anyone, old man." He stomped his foot and pointed at the group. "Hurry the hell up. We don't have all day."

The group started ambling toward the clubhouse at the sudden voice spike.

"Make sure he's comfortable in there, and do anything he asks you to. If he asks you to wipe his nose, I expect someone to be running with a tissue."

The group sped up from their casual pace to a more rushed stance before they disappeared inside the building.

"What do you make of the new prospects?" Richard asked.

"It's a little too early to say, but I like what I see. We'll see how they deal with the stress as we go. God knows they'll get plenty of that."

"True that." Richard slapped Lucien's shoulder. "Let's get inside. I'm cooking out here." He followed the mob inside to find Irving propped up at a nearby table and one prospect sitting across from him. "How's it feel being back, Irv?" Richard sat down beside him. He looked across the table. "Cory here hasn't given you any trouble yet has he?"

"He's a little slow, but no real complaints yet."

"Slow?" Cory reached up and scratched his tanned chin. "I don't remember that."

"That's because you fell asleep in the hospital room, and I had to wake you up. Now go get me some water, prospect." Irving shifted his position with a groan.

"Come on, Ronald. Hurry up already." Cory's voice could be heard over at the bar.

"He seems like a good one, though maybe a little irresponsible," Irving said. "He reminds me a little of Skuz."

"That's trouble," Lucien chuckled.

"That doesn't mean you get to slack off either, Harold." Cory's voice at the bar carried over to the table.

"He does seem a little bossy. He looks like he might be

gunning for your position." Lucien turned his gaze to Richard. "You may need to nip that in the bud."

Richard looked over at the bar. "Hurry up, jackasses, and bring us a drink while you're at it."

Corey returned to the table with three full glasses of water sitting atop a tray. He placed it in the middle of the table.

"Well?" Richard asked.

Corey looked between the three and raised an eyebrow.

"Dumbass, he's injured," Lucien said. "Place it in front of him. He can't risk ripping his stitches because you're too lazy to move it. Get him a straw while you're at it."

Cory hurried off behind the bar and rummaged through the different boxes held beneath the bar.

"It's kind of fun being on the other end, isn't it?" Irving asked.

"Now he's getting it," Lucien said. "You've got about eleven months before they can even be patched in, so enjoy the manual labor at your fingertips. They're at your disposal."

"Unless of course the club needs them. You understand?" Richard asked.

"Of course."

"Speaking of which, we need to vote on some things now that you're out." Richard looked longingly at the meeting room. "It's been over a month since we last had a vote."

Cory placed the water directly in front of Irving with a bendy straw in it. "Anything else?"

"I'm good. Now go clean up the storage room in the back," Irving said.

"Right." His shoulders slumped as he turned and headed down the hallway.

"He's getting the hang of it," Richard said.

"By the time I'm done, they'll have made the place spotless." Irving looked across the relatively open room. "Where are Garret, Skuz, and Tony?"

"They're out collecting." Lucien took a sip of water. "Well, Garret and Tony are. Skuz is just the driver since he's on probation. They should be back soon. It was just a bunch of local shops."

"Yeah. He and his old lady finally found a new apartment I heard." Richard leaned the chair back on its hind legs and balanced. "Combine that with the news that you were getting out today, and he was all smiles earlier."

"I do appreciate all the visits from everybody while I was cooped up in that bed. It helped me not go crazy. You really don't want to watch television all day. That'll make you go nuts."

"Enough about that antiseptic smelling place," Richard said. "You're free again."

"Relatively speaking. My range of motion sure isn't what it used to be."

"Good thing we have prospects to wipe your ass for you if need be," Lucien quipped. The group of three erupted into laughter.

The sound of motorcycles outside could be heard getting louder. They became deafening, and then the rumbling ended.

"Sounds like they're back." Richard got up and went to the door. He opened it and kept it open. "Get in here right now. We've got a special guest today."

"Is he back?" Garret's voice could be heard. He sidestepped Richard and smiled when he saw Irving. "It must feel nice not to have to piss in a bag anymore."

"It was liberating. Let's put it that way."

"I'm a little jealous," Skuz said, entering the building. "You had a hot nurse tending you at every beck and call. How many times did you get her to mess around with your junk?"

"Ignore him." Garret took a seat.

"Hey, sometimes that actually happens."

"Sure it does." Garret looked back at the door to see Tony talking in a hushed voice with Richard before closing the door. "Look who's back, Tony." Garret raised his hand and pointed at Irving.

Tony nodded at Richard and came to take one of the only two remaining seats. "Good to see you up and around again, brother."

"Let's not get too comfy out here." Richard approached the table and walked past it, heading toward the meeting room. "We have business to discuss." He cupped a hand around his mouth. "Ronald, Harold, get over here."

The two rushed from the bar over to the table.

"We're going in there." Irving jabbed a thumb over his shoulder. "Get me in there now."

The pair lifted him out of his seat and led the club into the chamber before sitting him gently down on the seat.

"Get out of here." Garret pushed the two out. "Go clean or something. We'll call when we need you again."

With the two prospects gone and everyone seated, Richard cleared his throat. "Alright, finally we're ready to finalize some things."

"I don't mean to delay, but I'm a bit behind the times here. What exactly are we voting on?" Irving asked with a raised hand.

"No worries," Garret said. "We're voting on our new alliance with the Outback Boys and the terms of the deal."

"Which are?"

"We supply them with our market of meth, and they provide muscle and protection when we need it."

"That's it?"

"No," Richard sighed. "Like any good group, they want more. To be precise, they want a cut of all our deals."

"Which we're sure as shit not doing," Lucien said with narrowed eyes.

"Right. They're just dick wagging. They know they won't get it. They have to try though, or they'd look weak."

"If we forget the tax, it sounds like a good deal to me."

"Exactly. So, let's vote. Who's in favor of allying ourselves temporarily with the Outback Boys until this cartel heat dies down?" Everyone raised their hand. "Motion passes. Now I just have to finalize the negotiations, and we're set."

"If you can ever truly be prepared for a green light on the club," Lucien said.

"The rumblings have been quiet," Tony said. "I've not heard anything about ES-15 since last month. Either they're laying low, or they're flying under the radar."

"They're not going to give up," Skuz said. He flicked an errant purple strand up out of his view. "We know that. It's just a matter of how many men are they going to send into the grinder?"

"They certainly don't have qualms about that," Garret said. "They have the entire South American continent to draw troops from."

"Then if they do show up, we'll just have to make it untenable to stay up north," Irving said.

"What does untenable mean?" Skuz asked.

Garret elbowed Skuz in the ribs. "It means it wouldn't be worth it, you moron."

"I knew that."

"Sure you did," Richard said. "For the time being, Irv,

you'll oversee keeping the clubhouse in check since you're still recovering. Everyone stay armed at all times. As Irv here can attest, you can never tell when something will happen." He banged the gavel on the wooden rest plate. "Meeting dismissed."

Tony got up and opened the doors. "Get in here."

Harold brushed away black locks of hair after he jogged over. His baggy plaid shirt hung over his wiry frame. "Yes?"

"What do you think?" Irving angled his head to look over his shoulder. "Meeting's over. Now hurry up."

"That was quick."

"Did we ask your opinion?" Tony asked from Harold's side. He pushed him away. "Just do what we say, and keep your dumbass thoughts to yourself."

"Yes, sir." He helped Irving up and escorted him back to the table in the main room.

Everyone filed out of the meeting area, some moving toward the bar, others toward the table with Irving.

Garret and Skuz sat down beside Irving on either side.

Garret scratched the back of his neck. "Sorry about not showing up at the hospital as often as I should have."

"You were house hunting with a woman," Irving said with a chuckle. "It couldn't be helped. Speaking of which, where is Ann? I haven't seen her yet."

"She's on her way here now, if I know her."

"I still think it's a bad idea dating her," Skuz said.

Garret rolled his eyes. "Coming from you, I'll take that as an endorsement. By the way, you did stop going out with Jerry's sister, right?"

"Kind of hard not to, considering they were both locked up."

"Damn, for what?" Irving asked.

"What do you think?" During that raid they found all

sorts of explosives in the house. He's doing serious time. The last I heard, his lawyers are trying to take it from life without parole to a plea deal of thirty years. She's looking at ten years I believe."

Irving whistled. "Damn. You got out of it?"

"The forensics saw the cut marks on her arms. I'm cool." Skuz ran a hand through his bright purple mohawk.

"I guess that's one option down the drain in the future, unless you know another bomb maker."

"I'm not quite so lucky," Garret said. "I don't think that will be a problem though."

"Why?"

"The Outback Boys are notorious for having the best explosives. If we wanted, we could maybe negotiate for some access. It'd probably cost a pretty penny though."

"Better than not having access I guess."

The front door of the clubhouse shot open. A feminine voice floated inside. "I got it. Everyone get ready for..." Ann's blonde hair poked out from the side of the towering cake. "Ah poo, he's already here. I was hoping to surprise him."

"You shouldn't have."

"Nonsense." Garret showed a toothy smile. "Getting out of the hospital is worth celebrating after all."

"I can't argue with that."

"Don't get too loaded, boys." Richard stuck a finger into the icing and had his hand slapped away by Ann. He licked the icing off his finger. "We still have a meeting to attend with the Outback Boys later."

A few hours later...

"This place brings back memories." Richard overlooked the vast quarry below him. Piles of rock adorned the wide-open space below. "Remember?"

"I remember plenty about that day, least of which is this place. I was mainly focused on the sicario chasing me through the woods until you blew his leg off."

"Damn, Rich," Garret laughed. "I didn't know you had it in you."

"I had Enrique's grenades is what I had." He turned away from the precipice and walked back toward the line of motorcycles. "Are they always this late?" He brought his wrist up and looked at his watch.

"They'll be here." Skuz leaned against a nearby tree.

Garret pulled out a cigarette from his vest's front pocket, extracted one, stuck it between his lips, and pulled out a lighter from his jeans. "How the hell would you know?" He flicked the lighter until a small flame jumped out and engulfed the edge of the white stick. Puffs of smoke escaped his lips.

"In the interest of diplomacy, I did a little digging."

"We're in trouble now if he's our negotiator," Tony smirked.

"Screw you, man." Skuz reached down, grabbed a pebble, and chucked it toward Tony. "Anyway, I have insurance that they'll show up. That dude will want his money."

"For what exactly?" Richard asked.

"Just a little moonshine."

"How exactly were you planning on transporting that back to the clubhouse on your bike?"

"I'm glad you asked." Skuz kicked off the tree and moved to his bike. He opened the trunk on the back. "Looks normal, right?"

"Get to the point."

He reached inside and, one click later, a hidden compartment opened in the bottom.

"I'll be damned," Richard said, leaning forward and inspecting the newfound space.

"It's amazing the things you'll put your effort into, boy." Lucien shook his head.

Garret raised a hand above his eyes and squinted into the distance. "Ignoring our moonshine boy, I think they're here." He pointed down the path to see a small caravan of cars heading toward them.

Richard raised the binoculars hanging around his neck and looked through. "That's them alright. I'll do the talking." He lowered them and looked at Skuz. "Got it?"

"Of course, Pres."

The cars rumbled up the dirt and gravel path until they stopped behind the line of bikes. A group of six men filed out between the two vehicles. All of them were visibly armed with wide smiles on their faces.

"Rich, it's been a long time since I've seen you," the leading one said.

"Eric, it's been too long." Richard met him in the middle. The two wrapped their arms around each other and patted their backs before taking a step back.

"You crazy bastard, what did you get yourself into this time? I heard it had to do with ES-15?"

Richard scratched his stubble clad chin. "Yeah, we're not on good terms after last month's fiasco."

"We were big fans of your work. Those savages and their subsidiary gangs have been encroaching on our turf. Seeing you boys send them temporarily back across the border gave us some breathing room."

"So, what's with asking for a cut of our action then, buddy? That doesn't seem fair."

"You know how business is. You need to look after your own." He turned to his side. "Speaking of which, let me introduce you to my men." He pointed to a tall built man in a wifebeater and jeans. His sunglasses and shaved head created an imposing figure. "This here is my second in command, Mr. Kelly. Don't make fun of his name if you know what's good for you."

He bent at the waist and bowed. "Nice to meet you. I'm in charge of defense and will probably be working in close conjunction with your defense coordinator."

Garret stepped forward and offered a hand. "Guess we'll be working together then. I'm Garret Price."

Kelly didn't respond verbally but merely took his hand, squeezed, and shook it before backing up into the line.

"The guy to his left is in charge of our operations."

A stocky raven-haired man stepped past Kelly and nodded his head. "I'm Walter. I'll be in charge of overseeing the deliveries between us."

"Nice to meet you," Richard said. "Now let's nail down the finals of our arrangement."

"We want unfettered access to as much junk as we can move."

"We can make that happen. Just let us know how much you need. We'll make sure our suppliers are up to the task, so long as it's within reason. We don't have as many smurfs as we used to. We'll also need access to your heavier fire-power, for a fair price of course."

"We'll need at least a pound a week to make that work."

Richard paused for a moment. "Yeah, we could make that happen. Now to be clear, you're not getting a cut of our profits."

"So long as you get the stuff to us on time, that's fine."

Eric extended a hand which Richard took immediately. "Deal."

"I'm happy we could come to an arrangement."

"Do you hear that?" Garret asked.

"What is that?" Kelly asked. "It sounds like a helicopter. They shouldn't be coming all the way out here. The border's at least thirty miles away."

"I don't think that's border patrol." Garret's eyes widened as he saw a helicopter come into view. "Get to cover now!" He pushed Kelly and Skuz toward the nearby forest.

Everyone scattered into the nearby woods as a whirring noise approached. Dirt shot up from the shots landing in the soil where they once were. The dilapidated building collapsed as bullet holes riddled the decrepit wooden supports. Clouds of dust enveloped the entire area.

"Is that a motherfucking attack helicopter?" Garret asked.

"It sure isn't a medical transport." Richard dove behind a nearby boulder. "I guess they found us."

"Does anyone have a plan besides huddling up and hoping we don't die?" Skuz asked, curling against the tree he found himself behind.

"We don't have rpgs, if that's what you're asking." Eric held his hands over his ears. "I didn't think they'd have a fucking chopper at their disposal. I'll make sure we're ready next time."

"Just keep your heads down," Richard said.

Another louder roaring made itself known above them. A monstrous explosion above them drew their eyes upward. They saw a jet zoom past the fiery explosion above. Hunks of metal went flying, embedding themselves in the various trees and surfaces. A burned arm fell in front of Skuz, causing him to let loose an involuntary scream.

"Jesus Christ," Richard said. "Is everyone alright?" He stayed behind cover and peeked around. "I think it's over."

"What in the world was that? One of your associates?" Skuz asked Eric.

"Not us. The cartel had to have flown that attack heli over the border. If I had to guess, it was the local air base. Speaking of which, we need to bail right now. They've no doubt called this in. This area is going to be swarming with feds soon."

"At least they were aiming at us, not the bikes." Garret knelt beside his and ran his hand over it. "Let's figure this shit show out later. We need to get out."

"Agreed," Eric said. "Deal's on, and brother, we want retribution just as much as you do now. They fucked with the wrong boys this time."

"Music to our ears."

Garret jogged over to Skuz and pulled him up. "Come on, man. We've got to get out of here. Ignore that. It's just an asshole's burnt arm."

"It just surprised me is all." Skuz dusted himself off and hopped onto his bike.

"We'll talk later. Everyone inside the cars. We're out." He watched everyone else from his group file inside before taking the last seat. He stuck his head out of the open window. "We'll talk tonight. Don't worry, we'll be ready next time. Count on that."

"Of that I have no doubt." Richard mounted his bike and revved the engine. "Now let's go home."

2

_____

"Are you serious?" Ann asked. "I should have been there."

"No offense, but I doubt you could have done much. It was pretty much duck and hope you don't get your head, legs, or other limbs blown off."

"I knew they wouldn't give up, but that's beyond my predictions." Ann used the spatula and flipped the sizzling hamburger. "I'm going with you next time."

"The hell you say," Garret said from in front of the refrigerator.

"Do you remember a month ago when we gave this a go? I'm not your typical old lady, and you need to accept that."

"It doesn't mean I have to like it."

"No, it doesn't. Besides, I'm getting a little bored playing the good wife back here. I need a little action."

"Action you say?" Garret wrapped his arms around her waist and nuzzled his stubble clad chin into her neck. "I can help with that part."

"Get off of me." She shook him off. "Don't do that when I'm cooking, unless you like burned meat."

He took a step back with a smirk. "Okay, have it your way. Just don't blame me if you get hurt. I'm just trying to stop that, as the good boyfriend."

"I appreciate it, but it's not warranted. I could probably take you down anyway, young buck. Don't forget, I used to have your job."

"We'll agree to disagree on that one."

A chirping filled the apartment.

"That's probably the boys." Garret patted Ann on the behind and watched her yelp and jump. "I'll go get that, dear."

"Jackass," she mumbled under her breath, returning her focus to the cooking in front of her.

Garret opened the door. "Well, if it isn't these bums at my new home." He stepped aside and let the procession into the main room.

Richard whistled. "Nice digs you two've got here."

"It must have cost a pretty penny," Tony said, helping Irving through the door. "Too bad it's only one bedroom."

"That's all we need," Garret said.

Lucien sat in the lone recliner in the room and rocked. "At least that's one more thing you don't have to worry about. Nobody knows where this is, besides us."

"If they burn this one down, I'm going to be pissed." Garret moved back to the open kitchen and took out plates from the cabinets, placing them on the bar. He placed empty hamburger buns on the plates. "You're all sure you weren't followed?"

"We doubled back three times," Irving said, sitting on the end of the couch. "What happened out there to make you so paranoid all of a sudden?"

"They sent a damned attack helicopter after us today,

brother," Skuz said to the man sitting next to him. "We were just damned lucky that jet fighter showed up."

"Keep shop talk to a minimum," Richard said, his voice stern.

"Oh please," Ann said slapping the juicy meat patties onto the buns already on the plates in front of her. "It's not like I haven't heard worse and helped your sorry asses out of said places."

"It's just a good habit to get into," Richard shrugged. "No offense intended. Loose lips sink ships."

"I can't argue with that. But try me. I may surprise you." Ann finished preparing the meal and trekked it over to the main dining table alongside Garret. "Meal's ready. Maybe you all can explain to little old me exactly what you're planning to do? I might have a genius idea." She laid the plates onto the table before sitting down herself.

The group got up and took their respective seats at the large dining table. Garret took a seat at the head of the table, with Richard sitting across from him and Ann to his right side.

"How would you have dealt with a fully armed assault helicopter then, beyond what we did - which was hiding and praying in a nearby wooded area?"

"You were half right." Ann ripped into the meat and licked her chin. "The helicopter wouldn't be able to follow you in there, but you needed a plan to neutralize it."

"Not to be a dick, but how exactly should we have done that?" Garret asked.

"You know the military's working on emp grenades, right? I heard they recently finished work on a prototype."

"Great, we should call them up and ask for a box," Skuz scoffed. "I'm sure they'd oblige us."

"Dumbass." Ann glared at Skuz. "Who do you think the

Outback Boys get their weapons through? Their army contacts, that's who. They don't need some heavy duty rpg, though that would also work. It'd be a lot lower key to simply knock it out of the sky."

"We'll keep that in mind for next time. Hopefully there won't be one." Richard took a big drink of water. "Besides, wouldn't that cause a big uproar if some big new secret tech went missing? It seems like more trouble than it's worth."

"You'd have to ask them. They're the ones with the contact. I was just floating an idea so you wouldn't be as conspicuous carrying around a damned rocket propelled grenade launcher on the off chance another helicopter comes after you."

"If they got one," Garret said, "they can get another."

"It does no good to worry about that right now." Richard finished eating his burgers and pushed the plate away. "We need to set up our delivery pipeline soon. We won't see any hardware until after our first delivery, and we need those weapons."

"We have one pound and some change in stuff. The first delivery won't be a problem, but the subsequent deliveries might. We barely have enough smurfs to produce a pound a week."

"Can we though?" Irving asked. "As long as we can, that's all that matters."

"If even one smurf backs out, we're fucked," Skuz sighed. "They get squirrelly all the time. It means we'll either have to convince them not to give up their extra job or find new ones."

"Yeah, I wasn't in the drug trade." Ann picked up the assorted empty plates and placed them in the sink. "What's a smurf exactly?"

"Someone who goes to stores to buy cough medicine for

meth. Usually you get carded and have to sign. It causes a lot of them to get nervous that they'll be on the hook and spend a few decades in a state penitentiary if we're ever caught," Tony said. "We pay them well for their time, but they still get nervous just buying cough medicine every week."

"I imagine so with the way they've been cracking down on that stuff."

"Assuming we can keep up our production," Richard started, "we'll need a volunteer to mule it to their location of choice.

"A young man in his early twenties in a kutte probably wouldn't be a very good mule." Ann finished cleaning up the remaining plates. "A young woman with a history of smuggling and keeping her cool in the face of danger would have a far better chance."

"She has a point," Lucien said. "It's not like the Outback Boys are going to be able to intimidate her either."

"I could also take Irving here and make it a bit of a trip. He could get some excitement and not just stay cooped up in the clubhouse all day, if he'd like?" Ann looked toward Irving.

"Anything's better than sitting with the prospects all day. They're nice enough, but damn are they annoying. Always asking questions and complaining."

"It's settled then, assuming you boys sign off. I'll get your deliveries where they need to be. I give you Ann's patented promise." She held up her index finger and middle finger together. She winked and blew an air kiss. "I always get my cargo where it's going, or your money back."

"I'd be more worried about you then I would the cargo." Garret looked away from the group when he heard a series of laughs and hisses.

"Aw, that's cute." Skuz reached over and grabbed Garret's cheek. "He's worried about his girl."

"I appreciate the concern, dear, but I've got this."

Garret shook off Skuz's grip. "I believe that."

"With the delivery status settled, the only thing left is the smurfs. Is there any one that's getting flaky?" Richard asked

"I know one guy who's been asking to quit for the last week. You want I should go over there and convince him to continue?" Skuz asked.

"Someone should," Lucien said. "Just not you. We need someone who has a little more charm and persuasion."

"I've got charm oozing out of my very pores."

"I don't think that's what that is," Irving said. A round of chuckles erupted from around the table. "I think that's sweat, judging by the smell."

"You're lucky you're on the mend, or I'd punch you one."

"I can always go if you think it'd be better," Garret offered. "At least I'm not under as much scrutiny as you. You need to stay low until your legal troubles pass by."

The corner of Ann's lips perked up. "In my experience, a feminine touch can get men to commit all manner of nonviolent crimes. I'd imagine I could help get him to buy some cold medicine," Ann said.

"Good idea," Garret said. "If anyone can get a man to do anything, it'd be you. I'll go as backup - just in case."

"It's settled," Richard said. "Now what do you two do around here for fun besides the obvious?"

"You need to see the setup I made for my weapons collection." Garret stood and pointed down a nearby hallway.

"Oh Lord, not the cabinet again," Ann said.

"You can't just leave it at that," Irving said. "I need to see this."

"It's just a false back to the cabinet, but I guess you men get excited over this crap."

"Damned straight." Lucien helped Irving up. "A man needs to defend his weapons. You never know when you might need them."

"Alright, old man. Anyone who's interested follow me." Everyone except Richard trailed behind Garret as he led them back into their bedroom.

"You know you don't have to volunteer to do this for us," Richard said, kicking back against the table and balancing the chair.

"I'm getting a bit stir crazy just sitting here. I need something to do. If it helps us get out from under the cartel, all the better. I need to pull my weight too. This is right in my wheelhouse, so don't worry. Even if the police pull me over, they'll never find the stuff. I hid a human from border patrol. I can certainly hide a small one-pound package from deputies."

"If I didn't believe you could do it, I'd get someone else. That's not what I'm worried about."

"Aw, are you saying you finally trust me?"

"Don't put words in my mouth." Richard crossed his arms. "I'm just looking out after my sergeant-at-arm's old lady. That's all. It's my duty."

"Sure that's all it is? Why can't you men just admit when you're trying to be nice?"

"It's a mystery of the world that you women will never understand."

"Really? That's what you're going with?"

"You heard me."

Ann rolled her eyes. "Whatever. It's a wonder you boys get any business done with that kind of attitude."

"I'll text you the drop off address when I get it. You might want to prepare whatever vehicle you're going to use. You do have one, right?"

"Of course, I do. Did you think I didn't own a vehicle when we first met? The only reason I never had it was because you all were keeping me pseudo prisoner. After that debacle, I went and retrieved it. You might have noticed the white low rider outside? That was mine. It's already fitted with plenty of hiding places big enough to fit a man if I wanted to. You never know when that'll come in handy."

"Just make sure you're not out of practice, and don't get too cocky."

"I appreciate the sentiment, but with all due respect I've done more smuggling jobs than your entire charter to date. I'll get it there."

"Just be prepared for their unique mannerisms when you get there. Try not to take them too seriously."

"What?" Ann asked.

"You'll see for yourself."

Ann's nose crinkled up. "I hope for their sake they know how to keep their hands to themselves."

"Yeah, Garret wouldn't appreciate that." Richard peeked at her out of the corner of his eye. "Seriously, we need them, so control yourself."

"I got it."

"Now let me go see exactly what all the hubbub is about." Richard pushed the wooden seat across the floor with a screech and got up. He walked through the door the rest of the group went through and found them huddled around a wooden cabinet sitting next to the bed. "Alright now, let me see this."

The crowd parted, leaving only Garret in front of the cabinet. He motioned Richard over. "How about it? What do you think?"

"It looks like a regular drawer that you open up. Where's the payoff?"

"Ah, I knew you'd ask that." He reached inside and pushed a button and an audible click filled the room. "Behold." He pulled his hand out and this time, instead of a cabinet full of clothes, a drawer filled with pistols was pulled out instead. He leaned forward, inspecting the handiwork. "You need to show me how you did that. That's much better than a false bottom."

"The best part is, unless you know where the button is, it's just a regular drawer. You'll never find the cache unless you know it's there."

"Damned nice," Lucien grunted. "If you're not careful you're going to end up with a new side job."

"Yeah," Tony said. "I could use one myself. You never know when it could come in handy."

"I'd be up for it. It wouldn't take that long, now that I know how it all works. You'll be paying for materials though."

"Before you start gathering clients for your new carpeting gig, how about you focus on more pressing matters?"

"No doubt." Garret shut the drawer to another click. "I'll get Ann, and we'll go convince the smurf to take a trip to the drug store. Just give us an address, and we'll be going."

Tony retrieved a crumpled piece of paper from his pants pocket and handed it to Garret. "This is the guy. He's a worry wart, so put your kid gloves on."

"Be careful on your way back. I want you to take someone with you two, just in case."

"I'm your man," Skuz said.

"Not you." Richard pushed Skuz back a step. "You've got an impending court case coming up. You can't afford to get mixed up in this shit. I was thinking more like Lucien or Tony. Either of you two up for it?"

"Aw come on, Pres," Skuz whined, "I can be good."

"Wouldn't that be the day?" Lucien asked. "I'll go and make sure they don't get themselves in too much trouble."

"Your confidence in us is astounding, old man," Garret said.

"Not so much in you, but I am confident ES-15 might try something. They obviously haven't forgotten before."

"Maybe if we're lucky Eric will have secured some firepower. Should we swing around and grab some extra stuff just in case?" Garret asked.

Richard rubbed his stubble laden chin. "I'll call and see. I doubt he would have gotten his hands on some so soon, but considering they were shot at too, it wouldn't surprise me if they put a rush on it." He pulled out his phone and dialed a number. "Eric, how are you doing, buddy?"

"As well as can be expected given what happened today. What's up?"

"Just wondering if you found some of your supplies already. If you had, I was going to send an extra gift for you."

"Anxious for your new toys already? I can't say I blame you. Yeah, we got a little something to show you."

"I'll make sure to send that extra gift then. Where should we drop off our gift?" He pointed at a notepad sitting on the nearby table and snapped his fingers. He dug into his pants and pulled out a pen while Garret tossed him the pad. He bent over and recorded the information being relayed. "Got it. It's always a pleasure doing business. I'll send my best over right away." He pushed the paper over to Garret who snatched it up.

"I can't wait to see who you're talking up. That's a rare

sight. Send them over. We'll show them the proper hospital-ity. Talk to you later, buddy."

"Later, man." Richard folded up the phone and returned it to his pants pocket. "It's on. Gather all the meth. All pound and a half. We'll need it for the deal."

"What about next week?" Lucien asked. "At the current rate, we only create a pound a week. We don't have enough cough medicine to make it any quicker."

"We'll deal with that next week. So long as we have a full pound the alliance is solid," Richard said. "For now, we need a way to defend ourselves if they send more air rein-forcements."

"I can't argue that. I think my life flashed before my eyes when we were dashing for the tree line earlier." Lucien placed a hand over his chest.

"Must have been quite the long experience." Skuz laughed until Tony slapped the back of his head and stopped him.

"There'd be no greater pleasure than to take their best and slap them back down. If they send another helicopter, we shoot it down. It'd send a real message... that we don't take shit in any form."

"I guess we'll take your car then, dear," Garret said. "We should get going."

"Come on, you bums." Richard beckoned the group. "Let's get out of here and prepare a storage spot for our new goodies."

"Sounds fun," Irving said, hopping on his one good foot toward the door. "I need to go make sure those damned prospects aren't jacking around anyway. It'll be a good excuse to get them working again."

"That's a good idea." Lucien's hand grasped the door-knob. "Let the kids do the heavy lifting. Let's go, boys. We've got work to do after that fine meal." He looked at Ann and nodded his head with a serene smile.

"At least someone here appreciates my talents."

"Wasn't that the second time you'd ever actually cooked though?" Garret asked before an elbow found its way into his solar plexus. He rubbed his abdomen and smiled. "It was good though. What was that for?"

"You're clueless." Richard shook his head and led the group out of the apartment.

Later in Ann's car...

Ann opened the back door and leaned inside. She pushed a camouflaged button on the side of the middle arm rest. She lifted the top off, reached inside, lifted another compartment out, and stashed the package inside before reassembling it. "There we go. We're ready."

"At least the cook had it ready for us this time. I guess Lucien's threats last time put the fear of God in them. He didn't even argue."

"He probably heard about your beef with the cartel and doesn't want to get involved, if I had to guess. Besides, it's always better to not ask questions. Maybe he finally figured that out."

Garret sat down in the passenger seat and put it in the reclined position as Ann got in on the driver's side. "We're not too far from their place actually. If all goes well, we'll be home before long."

"Do you know a lot about these guys you've allied with?"

"They're a medium sized club that we have history with. They have presence across the country, but mostly here in the tristate. Our older guys used to be well associated with their shot callers in neighboring states. Lucien and their charter president were in the marines together. I heard he kept him alive after an unlucky artillery strike. Our groups have been uneasy allies since. We keep out of their way and vice versa."

"Since they have military ties, that's how they get their weapons then."

"You got it," Garret said. "I don't know how, and I don't want to. That's their business. We prefer the slightly less dangerous drug game, not weapons."

"They're both radioactive, but yeah, I get it. They're big earners."

"Like peanut butter and chocolate, they go together too well. Just one piece of advice - don't take anything they might say to you too seriously. They're not as polite as us sometimes, especially on their home turf."

"I'm pretty sure I can handle rude men," Ann murmured. Her eyes danced up to the rear-view mirror. "Fuck. Don't look now, but I think we have an admirer."

Garret peeked at the mirror to his right. "I guess we're going to see how good you really are." He leaned over and kissed her cheek. "Don't disappoint me now."

"Just stay quiet and be amazed then." She pushed him away with an arrogant grin. She pulled over to the side of the road when the sirens blared from the cop car behind them. "Just don't move your hands, and don't look at the compartment. We'll be fine. Stay calm. I've got this." She rolled down the window as the siren faded away.

"Morning, ma'am," the male officer's gaze moved to Garret and narrowed. "Sir. Do you have any idea why I pulled you over today?"

The corner of Ann's mouth curled upward. Her voice

changed to a higher pitched, sweeter tone. "I'm sorry, Officer. I can't say that I do."

"I'm going to need to see your license and registration, ma'am."

"Right away." Ann dug into her pants pocket, retrieved the rectangular identification card, and handed it to the man. She leaned over toward the glove compartment and opened it, digging around until she yanked out a white paper labeled vehicle registration, then handed it over.

His eyes zoomed left and right. He talked as he read. "Are you aware you were going fifty-five in a thirty-five area?"

"Oh gee." Ann lifted a single finger to her lips. "I'm like really sorry, Officer. I had no earthly idea. I'd never intentionally speed."

"What about your friend here?" He leaned against the window and peered inside at Garret. His eyes narrowed as they traced his figure. "What's your story? Judging by that colorful jacket, I can guess."

Garret remained quiet and merely avoided the officer's gaze.

"Regardless, I'm going to have to give you a ticket. I can't change the laws." He pulled out a small white pad. His other hand pulled out a pen tucked in his breast pocket, and he scribbled. "I don't know what you two were hurrying toward, but I recommend you cool it."

"Of course, Officer. Again, I'm really sorry about this." Ann's eyes were glued to her lap, and her lip quivered.

"Be that as it may, make sure you pay this off and this will all go away." He ripped a piece of the white paper away and handed it to Ann. "If not, this just gets worse - so don't forget."

"I sure won't. Have a good day, Officer, and be careful."

"Yeah," the officer walked off, "you too."

Ann rolled the window back up. "Fucking dick." She watched the police cruiser pull into traffic on her left, put on a sugary sweet smile along with a wave, and started her own engine. "I hate those self-righteous twat waffles."

"You could have fooled me with that performance. I mean that in the nicest way."

She pulled off the side of the road and back into traffic. "Deputies are nothing compared to border patrol guards. Those people take their jobs too seriously. These rank and file blue drones are too susceptible to having their egos played to. All you have to do is be polite, act cute, be apologetic, and you're generally fine. We were okay until he saw your gang colors, and even then..." She pumped the brake as they approached a red light. "You did the right thing by not answering."

"Check it out." Garret snapped his fingers. He jabbed a thumb toward the window beside him. "I think he's following us, or planning to."

Ann glanced over. "We'll see. Try not to be obvious and watch him. I have an idea if he is."

The green light lit up, and Ann pressed the gas pedal. She turned to the left. Garret leaned to his left and gazed at the rear-view mirror. "He's definitely following us, sweetie. What's your plan?"

"We can't drag a cop to a deal site. We'll have to get rid of him. How do you feel about a little food before we drop by?"

"They're sticklers for punctuality, but I guess we don't have a choice here," Garret said.

She flicked the lever in front of her and a clicking filled the cabin as her foot stepped on the brake. She turned into the parking lot. "He won't sit outside all day. We'll go get an ice cream, and he'll be gone I bet by the time we get out."

The two got out of the car and headed inside the nearby shop. Garret stood by the door and kept periodically peeking outside while Ann headed up to the counter. "That's right. We're just on a date," he whispered.

"One chocolate cone and one rainbow cone please," Ann's voice droned in the background.

"There we go." Garret watched the police car pull off from its parking space across the street.

"Did it work?" Ann asked, kicking his shins.

"Ah," Garret snapped back to her. "Yeah, he just left. We may as well treat this as a date though." He pushed open the door, led the two outside, and extended his arm to the nearby table. He pulled out a seat. "Please."

"Aren't you the gentleman." Ann took the seat. She licked the chocolate cone. "He was probably after you, you know. It wasn't me. I guarantee it."

"Sorry about that. You know protocol as well as I do."

"Colors aren't optional when you're representing the club. Yeah, I know. It just can complicate things. That's why you have my expertise, to pull your ass out of the fire."

Garret took a bite out of his cone. "I'm more worried about the fire we've ignited by being late."

"They'll deal with it." Ann took the last bite of her cone and wiped her face with the provided napkin. "They're adults."

"You say that now. We'll see." Garret got up and finished his snack. "At least we're nearby." He threw his arm around her shoulders. "Just leave the talking to me when we get there."

"Don't trust me?" she asked, looking at him.

"We all have our strengths and weaknesses. You deal with the subterfuge - I deal with the diplomacy with allies. It's just how it goes."

"Just because you're right, doesn't mean you say it in a nice way. You need to work on that."

"Have you ever dealt with Aussies before?" Garret asked, getting into the passenger seat.

"They're not different than any other gang I bet."

Garret laughed out loud. "I can't wait to see this."

Outback Boys Base of Operations...

Garret pushed open the car door and led the two toward the walled off compound. "Hey, lads. Sorry for the wait, but we're here."

A shuffling inside accompanied a tiny slit opening in front of them in the middle of the gate. "You're late," a voice with an Australian accent said. "What took you so long, you bogan?"

"I don't know what that means, jackass, but open the door. We've got your gift."

The peep hole closed. A clink of metal preceded the low rumble. The giant blue gate slid to the side. "Go ahead then, Drongo," the voice said. "Get inside already."

"You're lucky I'm not familiar with Australian lingo, or I'd kick your ass." Garret led the two inside and smirked at the gatekeeper to their immediate left.

"Garret Price. It's always good to see you, ya cunt." Garret saw a familiar face extending a hand toward him while another man shut the gate behind them.

Garret accepted the handshake. "Sorry about being late. We had a bit of a delay on the way over, but we took care of it."

"Who's this?" Kelly raised a black eyebrow as his neck

bent back to look up at Ann. "Christ! Sheila's built like a brick shit house, isn't she?"

"What the fuck did you call me?" Ann growled and stomped forward until she was stopped by a gentle palm from Garret.

"I think he just called you tall. Ease up," Garret said.

"Sore spot for you, Sheila?"

"No, I'm just not used to being compared to an outhouse. You Aussies must be a little uncultured to call a lady that."

Kelly released a deep laugh. "Easy, girl. I can tell I'm going to like you already.

"Just don't try to keep pissing her off. She knows how to take care of her own business."

"If she's with you, I don't doubt it," Kelly said. "Sorry, Sheila."

Ann nodded without saying anything further. She folded her arms in front of her and narrowed her eyes toward Kelly. "Don't call me Sheila."

"Pour yourself a glass of cement then." Kelly chuckled to himself. "Come on inside. There's no sense jawing the arvo away out here in this heat." He led the pair toward a small building behind the main structure. "Walter should be inside waiting." He pointed to the building a few yards ahead. "I have to get back to keeping watch. I think you'll be pleased by that beauty." He took a few steps. "If you'll excuse me, Sheila." He jogged off back toward the gate.

"That guy annoys me." Ann followed his retreating form before turning back to the building.

"It's just their lingo. Like I said, leave the talking to me." Garret pushed the structure's door open and led the way inside.

The small building housed a huge rectangular table. Assorted shelves lined the walls on every side with tools of all kinds hanging and sitting, just waiting to be used. A lone light dangled above the table swaying left and right. Walter had both of his hands leaning against the table with a giant brown box sitting in front of him. He looked up at the two and smiled. "Welcome, you two. I heard you were coming bearing gifts, so I did as well."

Garret reached inside his jacket and produced the bag. "Of course. A pound and a half, exactly as we agreed on. Weigh it if you like, it's all there." He tossed the bag on top of the illuminated table.

Walter turned around and grabbed a small grey electronic scale. He pressed a button and threw the package on top. He leaned down and squinted his eyes. "It's slightly heavier, weighing in at one point six pounds."

"We always aim to please our allies when we can."

"Deadset. We do too." Walter removed his glasses and used his shirt to rub the glass. He tore open the top of the cardboard box. He pushed the container across the table. "Go ahead. Look at them beauties."

Garret pulled the box over and peered inside. "What are these?" He pulled out a small black cylinder.

"That, mate, is the ridgy-didge. It's an electro-pulse grenade. You know of EMP technology? That is cutting edge tech that we got at a discount. We pass the savings onto you, the dear consumer." Walter put his thick frames back on. "Now you can take out any vehicle nearby. Just pull the pin, chuck one of these beasts beneath it, and watch its engines and battery drain before your very eyes. It's got quite a range on it too if that pesky vehicle is in the air. Just be sure not to let it loose near your bike or it'll drain its battery too. I'd say the radius of this thing is a few hundred feet. You can throw that far, right?"

"I'm not going to ask how you got these." Garret examined the handheld weapon. "Just know that I'm impressed. This is next level tech. I didn't even think the US army had this yet."

"Bonza, so you like it?" Walter asked.

"I love it. How many are in here?"

"We gave you the mate's rate and loaded you up with five to start you out. Normally a pound and a half would only get you three. They are expensive, don't you know? You shouldn't need more than that anyway, unless they send a bloody squadron after us next time. If they try that again, you'll cark them for sure, eh, you bastard?"

"If that means kill, you're damned right, sir." Garret had a toothy smile as he rotated the cylinder, inspecting it by the lone light source in the room.

"They'll shit their striders when they realize you have that. I guarantee it."

"Ann, dear," he placed a hand on her lower back and rubbed, "could you go get the car? We need to load these up away from prying eyes."

"Just tell Kelly to let you in. They'll answer to old Walter if those cunts give you any trouble."

"I'll pass on the message," Ann nodded. "I'll be right back, boys." She threw open the door and closed it behind her.

"How in the bloody hell did you manage to land a lass like her?" Walter locked eyes with Garret. "She's as tall as a basketball player and built like a warrior."

"Probably because she used to be in a lady's gang with the same job as me." He pointed to the Sergeant-at-Arms patch on his chest.

Walter whistled. "She was the enforcer too? How'd you end up with a tough broad like her? She seems to have kangaroos loose in the top paddock if you know what I mean."

"She's a little crazy."

"Don't tell me you've turned into a root rat like your boy, Skuz was it? He was always hunting for a good shag, wasn't he?"

"You don't know the half of it." Garret placed the hand-held weapon back in the box. "That idiot is always chasing a skirt at the most inopportune times."

"Well, you and the missus will be fine by my measure," Walter said. "If I might be so bold, what's your plan after you get these back to your clubhouse?"

"That's a club decision. I don't know how you boys do it, but we're a democratic council of sorts."

"Right, you motorcycle lads and your voting. I almost forgot. I'm too used to getting the mission and just doing it like a soldier."

"Nothing wrong with that if that's how you all work." Garret closed the box and placed it under his arm.

"I feel like I've seen her around here before," Walter said.

"You probably have. Her group used to be pretty big around here in the human trafficking gig. Maybe you've heard of the Valkyries?"

"Aye, I remember them. They kept to themselves mostly. Which furthers the question of how you snagged a goer like her. I bet your first meeting you cracked on her. Admit it."

"As I recall, during our first meeting she put a gun to Skuz's head before I did the same to show her my displeasure."

"You like to live dangerous. How do you know Sheila isn't still looking for revenge?"

"We've come to an understanding."

The door opened, revealing Ann. "An understanding about what now?"

"Guy talk. You don't need to know." Garret smiled, staring directly into her eyes.

"You two be careful on your way back now. Don't hesitate to call if something comes up, or if you need some extra bodies if you're going after those godless heathens. We're always up for a little revenge."

"We'll keep that in mind, my friend." Garret opened his arm and the two men stepped into an embrace. He stepped back and nodded. "We'll be heading out then. The same goes for you gentlemen. We're allies now, so don't be afraid to give us a ring if you need to."

"We'll give you a ring if those heathens come at us. They won't stand a chance now that we're prepared. Now be careful out there, and don't lose that box."

Garret patted the side of the brown container. "I'll keep it close."

"You'd best get your priorities straight." Ann grabbed Garret's ear and pulled him back toward the door, disappearing outside.

"Poor cuntstruck bastard." Walter shook his head with a wry grin and reached up to turn off the light.

3

"Gather round, gents." Garret plopped the brown package down on the bar. "I got us our answer to any more aerial assaults right here."

"Can that really take out a helicopter?" Tony leaned against the bar, staring at the unopened brown box. "I was expecting an rpg or something bigger."

"Most of the time size matters," Lucien said, "just not all the time. Spill it. What is in there?"

"I'm sure old man Lucien knows what emps are."

"Emp weapons are usually used only during nuke strikes as I recall," Lucien frowned.

Garret grinned and tore open the top of the box. "Yeah, but technology waits for no man." He reached into the box. "I present the future of emp technology." He pulled out one grenade and handed it over to Lucien. "That's handheld technology with a huge radius. If it's within a few hundred feet, its electronics are getting fried."

"Meaning we have the advantage, boys." Richard reached into the box and extracted one. "They won't know what hit them if they try something like that again."

"That's nice and all," Skuz said, "but what's our plan now? We can't just sit around and wait, can we?"

"It'd be asking to get hit again," Garret said, backing away from the bar. He looked over at Irving at the end of the bar near two of the prospects. "Hey, Irv. What do you think?"

"Going after the cartel ourselves is a fool's errand. We don't even know where they are posted up yet. We need more intel on them before we go on a more offensive footing."

"The only way to get that kind of information is having boots on the street or paying the right people. We'd be better off paying than putting manpower at risk," Lucien said.

"That presents its own risks." Richard placed the grenade back in the container. "If you talk to the wrong person, and he's on the take, then they'd know we're tracking them. What we need is a high-tech answer to a low-tech problem, and I have just the idea." His index finger came up and poked into the side of his head. "You just need to use your head and be a little sneaky. I'll need one volunteer for this to work."

"I'll go," Garret said. "What do I have to do?"

"We'll need to get a directional microphone, a decent camera, and some duct tape first. Next, it's unavoidable but we'll have to ask around the streets and be discrete. Once we know where they're holing up, we can perform a little absentee spying."

"Then first things first. Who are we asking?" Garret asked.

"If ES-15's barging up here, they have to be stepping on a lot of toes along the way. All we do is simply see what they know. See what the local hood rats know, and that'll give us a good idea where they are. They won't cause us any problems, and they'll gladly help us find them I bet."

"Good thinking," Garret said. "I know just the guy to ask. I'll have to look him up again."

"While he's doing that, Skuz, you're going shopping for what he needs."

"Forget that. I need to go with him, or have you forgotten we're in a war, Pres?"

"Fine, the rest of us will go get the tools, while you two go see what the locals know. Make sure they know the stakes of what's going on," Richard said. "If we win, the status quo continues. If the cartel does, their little business will be squashed, their families killed, and they'll be stuffed in a shallow grave. I bet that will convince them."

"I'll keep that in mind. In my experience though, honey usually works better. But if I need some vinegar, I'll remember that."

"Lucien, Tony, you're with me. We're going shopping. If you two run into any trouble, call us immediately. We won't be too far away." Richard took one of the electro pulse grenades and tossed it to Garret. "Take this. You never know if it'll be useful."

Garret bobbled it before finally catching it. "It'd be better than getting into a shootout on Main Street I suppose. A traffic jam's better than an innocent catching a bullet."

"Damned straight," Lucien said. "We're the defacto protectors of the community before the cops. Back in my day, people would come to us with their problems, and we'd take care of it. Not so much anymore."

"What are you talking about, old man?" Garret asked. "My old lady was one of them."

Lucien grumbled under his breath. "Anyway, be careful, watch your six, and keep your head down, boys."

"We're always the pinnacle of caution." Skuz dragged Garret away from the bar with a wide grin.

"They'll be fine," Richard said, watching the two exit the building. He glanced back at Lucien. "That's our cue to get moving too, unless you want to be out of position if anything happens."

"You'll be fine here?" Lucien asked Irving.

"Oh, you bet." Irving reached up his hand and snapped his fingers causing all three prospects to come running. "I have all the help I'll need here."

"Make sure to whip them into shape then," Lucien said. He and Richard headed for the door leaving only four men in the room.

"Gentlemen, we're going to be sure everything's spotless by time they all get back."

Harold groaned, scratching his bulging gut. "But, boss, we've been cleaning all day."

"Oh, I'm sorry," Irving said. "Did the prospect get too tired doing his duties? Suck it up. I'll help if you really need me to." He pressed his hands onto the bar and attempted to get up before Corey rushed over and stopped him.

"That's okay. You don't have to push yourself." He glared over at Harold's huge figure. "I'll start with shining the bar then."

"Fine," Harold said. "I'll go defrag the computer then while you all do the physical cleaning. That's just as important."

"Don't forget the anti-malware scan while you're at it, big guy." Irving smirked at Harold's huge form.

"I'll get the tables then," Ronald's quivering voice said as he slinked over to the middle of the room.

"You need to project more confidence, kid. That little voice you're using is just going to attract more trouble than it's worth. Act confident, even if you're not in the least. Believe me when I say you don't want to be singled out. I was when I was a prospect."

Ronald leaned over the table and wiped the surface with the cloth in his hand. "I'll take that under advisement." His voice was louder. "I just don't want to cause waves."

"That's a good attitude you've got there, but be bolder. Being the meek little sheep will only go so far. You'll be the club gopher until the next prospects show up like I was."

"You mean...?"

"That's right. I am practicing what I preach." Irving's eyes darted back behind the bar. "Hey, I saw that. No drinking on duty. You're running twenty laps around the clubhouse."

Corey hissed and hid the bottle behind him. "Seriously?"

"Get moving. Now! This isn't your own private brewery, jackass. Who do you think pays for that?"

"The club?"

"Which you're not paying dues into yet. Do you see the problem?" Irving lifted his hand and pointed out toward the front door. "Harold, keep him moving, and don't go easy on him."

Harold smiled. "Yes, sir." He marched over to Corey and grabbed his upper arm, yanking him toward the door. "I'll be counting how long it takes you to complete a lap. Don't even think of lazing around the back of the building, or I'll come back there and kick your ass."

"I love my new job." Irving kicked back on his stool and took another swig from the glass of water in front of him.

A little bit later in town...

Garret and Skuz pulled their bikes to the side of the road and stopped before taking off their helmets. Garrett readjusted his black leather kutte and scanned the street. "That's odd. Where is everyone?"

"They must be spooked or something," Skuz said. "This place is usually bustling with activity."

Garret pointed at a nearby multi-level house. "There's our target. Let's go see what's going on around here."

"Right behind you." Skuz followed and kept watch behind them.

Garret ignored the steps leading to the door and instead approached the connected garage. He knocked on the door with the back of his knuckles.

"What? Who is it?" a male voice asked.

"It's Garret, Jekyl."

"His name's Jekyl?" Skuz asked in a hushed voice.

"You chose Skuz as a nickname. I'm not sure you get to cast that stone," Garret whispered. He looked back at the garage. "Open the door, man. We mean no harm."

The garage raised with a clatter. A skinny young man ushered them inside. "Get in here already. Haven't you two heard?"

"Heard what?" Garret helped close the door. "What's happening here? Why is everyone inside or gone?"

"Word's traveled around that the cartel is going to be moving up here to Arizona. Everyone that has a hustle is trying to lay low and stay under their radar. No one wants to cross them except you. There are stories swirling around that you're in a war with them. Is that true?" Jekyl asked. "Surely not even the order would try and take them on. Right?"

"What's the latest news on the street on ES-15. Do they have any kind of local hangout that you've heard of?"

"Sure, everyone knows to stay away from that just opened tortilla restaurant downtown - except the normies. They flock to it due to the 'authentic Mexican experience' or whatever. No self-respecting criminal will go near there due to their reputation. It's just not worth it."

"Interesting," Skuz said. "How many are usually there?"

"Do I look suicidal? I have no clue. Weren't you listening? These guys don't mess around. In fact, if you do something stupid, you damned sure didn't get this from me."

"We'll keep your name out of it," Garret said. "Now tell us a little more about this restaurant. When do they open and close?"

"I've only drove past a handful of times." Jekyl walked back to the large sofa against the wall and sprawled out. His feet dropped to the concrete below. "I think it closes at ten p.m. Why?"

"Leave that to us. When does it open?"

"I think eleven a.m. I won't ask again, but I recommend you two stay away from them if you know what's good for you. I've heard stories about these guys, man. One guy got a little too curious and he's not around anymore, if you catch my drift."

"They killed him?" Skuz asked, examining a knickknack on the nearby cabinet space.

"Worse than that. I heard they cut his head off with a chainsaw, peeled his face off with a knife, and affixed it around a soccer ball. They left said ball on the steps of the school where the guy's kid went."

"Son of a bitch," Garret said. "You knew this guy?"

"He lived on this street since we were in grade school, but I never was friends with him or anything. We were more acquaintances. Still, I hear the kid's still in counseling sessions."

"No kidding." Skuz turned back to the group and paced back and forth in front of the nearby television. "Common courtesy would have been to at least leave the ball where only his wife would find it. Leave the kid out of it."

"I think you need to work on your sense of common courtesy," Jekyl said. "My point is, are you sure you two want to get involved with them?"

"Let's just say we're not afraid of reprisals from these savages," Garret said.

"I've told you where they are. Don't you two need to go plan your little suicide mission?"

"Just keep your head down and don't tell anyone you know us. You'll be fine," Skuz said. "They'll be gone from town before you know it."

"I doubt that, but can't deny I hope you boys succeed and drive them out. God himself knows it'd make the town a hell of a lot safer. The police haven't even tried to do anything. Probably because no one has called them. Normal folks just think the place is a mom-and-pop shop. See, they got some sixty-year-old couple to manage the place, probably under the threat of beheading if you ask me."

"Their family probably owed some money, if I were to guess," Garret said. "They probably have no real loyalty to the group. Still, we should assume they're working with them willingly, for safety's sake if nothing else."

"Yeah, whatever. Go be an action hero and get yourselves killed if you want. I'll stay here and eke out a living." Jekyl shuffled his feet across the smooth floor. "I don't suppose you all have any of that meth left? My supply has been running low lately, but the demand is as high as always."

"Can't help you there," Garret said. "We're fresh out. As you said, the market's slouching lately."

"Before we head out, I'm heading to the bathroom."

"Through the door, up the stairs, and it's the first door on your left." Jekyl pointed toward the nearby door leading inside the house.

Skuz disappeared into the building without further words.

"I'm surprised you're still around honestly. Word on the street was one of your members caught a bullet along with some shrapnel a month ago. The rumor swirling was that it was ES-15. Any truth to that?"

'What do you think?" Garret asked.

"I think that's why you're asking about them. You're at war, right?"

"You'd do best to keep that shit to yourself. The reason we're acquaintances is that I know you can keep a secret."

"Holy crap, it's true?" Jekyl's eyes bugged out. "Are you guys planning something?"

"You don't need to know that."

"You need to know anything else, dude? I want those assholes out almost as much as you do."

"Nothing else right now. If I need anything, do you mind if we come back?"

"Hey man, so long as you make sure they're not following you, I'll do whatever I can to help. I need to get back on the streets without worrying about getting my head lopped off by psychopaths from third world shitholes."

"I hear that." Garret leaned against the side of the sofa. "If I need help later, I know who to turn to." He reached into his back pocket and retrieved his wallet. He opened it, pulled out three one hundred-dollar bills, and placed them on Jekyl's chest. "For your trouble."

The door slammed upstairs along with thumps. The door leading into the garage busted open with Skuz standing there. "We ready to go or what?" Skuz asked as he bounded toward the garage door. "Did we get what we need?"

"Oh yeah." Garret kicked off the makeshift seat. "We'll talk to you later, Jack."

"Don't be a stranger now." Jekyl thumbed through the newfound bills, licking his lips.

Skuz bent down and jammed his fingers beneath the handle as he hefted the white aluminum garage door. He wiped the sweat from his brow after closing it back. "Did we get what we needed?"

"We got more than that," Garret said. "We got a new ally in case we need help. All for the low price of a little pocket change. He'll help us out. It's in his own financial best interest. Now let's head back and get the supplies. We'll go back to the club first. We'll need the van for this."

Outside the Restaurant...

"Where do you think I should set this up?" Garret asked Skuz beside him in the passenger seat.

"You're going to have a bit of trouble setting it up on a roof top unless it's abandoned. Saying that, height is an advantage. It also needs accessible wi-fi so it can transmit it's signal back to the clubhouse.

"It sounds like the only option I have is across the street beside the coffee shop then," Garret said. "The only problem is, I'm not sure they'd let me upstairs unattended. That's a damn newly refurbished office building."

"I guess you'll have to sweet talk your way through. Someone has to sit out here and set the damned thing up once you place it. I can't help you with your job too. I barely remember what all the prospect said myself."

"You're a huge help," Garret said. He grabbed the white plastic bag with one hand and the door handle with his other. "Guess it's show time." He exited the van and walked down the side of the street. He came to the glass doors and read the text on them. "Great, a lawyers office. Just who I want to try and convince to do me a favor." He saw a prim and proper desk with an employee sitting behind it. Two elevators were behind that. A few vending machines and a whole host of chairs lined the walls on the side.

He pushed open the door to hear the female voice greet him. "Welcome, sir. How may I help you today?" she greeted with a plastic smile. Her eyes wandered down to his leather kutte. "Oh, I see. Here for an appointment?"

"More like a tour, darling." He leaned forward onto the desk with a smile. "I need to know if these fellas, as good as they no doubt are, are right for me. You know?"

"I'm sorry, sir. Without an appointment you'll have to wait until one of them becomes available."

"Is that right? Well, I'd sure hate getting you in trouble, but I'm in something of dire straits right now. Can anything be done, Mrs?"

"It's Miss, and I don't think so, sir." She looked away, biting her lip. "I don't mean to be unkind. I'm just new on the job, sir."

"I understand. I don't mean to cause trouble, but I really need to see someone today. Is there anyway you can help me out? I'll pay extra for the walk-in fee if that would help. I don't mean to be trouble, but I'm in a bad way."

"Just take a seat over there, sir." She pointed to the empty row of seats. "I'll do what I can, so hold tight."

"I appreciate that, ma'am." He gave a warm smile and took a seat. He was looking out the window toward the van when the secretary interrupted him.

"Sir, I may have something." She beckoned him over with her hand. She placed a clipboard with a paper toward him. "Please sign your name first."

Garret took the pen and signed a fake name.

The woman took the clipboard back and waved over a security guard stationed outside the elevator. "Hey, take Mr. Garrison up to the third floor to see Mr. Walker."

"Yes, ma'am," the guard said. He looked over at Garret. "If you'll follow me, sir."

Garret got up and went over to the elevators with the uniformed security. "That was fast."

The guard let Garret get in first and followed him into the cramped space. His right hand reached forward and hit the third-floor button. The door closed, and he spoke up. "You're lucky. She normally slow-balls walk ins. You must have made an impression. With that getup, she probably knew you were in some hot water, eh?" He laughed.

Garret clicked his tongue. "Yeah. Cops seem to have a stick up their butt for us motorcycle enthusiasts."

The numbers above them chirped as the light switched from one to two. "Yeah, I'm sure that's why they have a problem with you," he said, smirking.

The third-floor indicator lit up with another chirp, and the doors opened. The guard went forward. "Follow me, Mr. Garrison." He led Garret through a well-lit, tiled hallway to a nearby waiting room. "Please wait here until Mr. Walker is ready."

"Thanks, man." Garret took the closest seat and watched

the security guard enter the elevator again. He looked across from him and saw another man reading a magazine from the communal table full of publications.

"You been here long?" Garret asked.

The man's body went rigid and he lowered the book. He peered over the pages. "At least twenty minutes so far."

"I guess that means I have time to head to the bathroom then." He got up and ambled out of the room. He looked down both sides of the hallway and saw a sign labeled stairwell beyond the bathrooms further down the hall. He ducked into the stairwell and began going up. He saw the door at the top. He pushed it open and saw a large air conditioning unit atop the building near the middle. He closed the door behind him.

"What are you doing here?" a figure to his side asked.

Garret jumped. "Jesus. You scared me."

A different security guard brought a cigarette to his mouth and inhaled. "Yeah, you're not supposed to be up here." He flicked the stub of a cigarette down to the floor and snuffed it with his heel.

"I doubt you are either."

"That's true. They want us to stop smoking up here. Is that why you're up here?"

"You caught me, dude." Garret placed the brown bag near his feet, reached into his vest's front pocket and pulled out the pack. "Want one?" He knocked the bottom of the pack causing one of the cigarettes to stick out toward the man. "It's on me - if you don't tell anyone about this."

"That goes for you too, buddy." The guard took a stick. "If they caught me up here, they'd fire me."

"Your secret's safe with me." Garret flicked his lighter and held it over the end of the cigarette. Smoke puffed from the end, and he removed it. He lit his own cigarette and stood side by side with the man staring out over the cityscape.

"These guys may be the best in town, but they're pains in the ass. Who are you here to see, if you don't mind my asking?"

"A Mr. Walker I believe."

"He's the worst among them. Be prepared for a nasty glare when he smells this on you." He held up the cigarette.

"Fuck him. I'm paying him."

The guard threw the remainder of the cigarette to the floor and crushed it. "Too true. Alright, thanks man. I need to get back to work before they fire me. Don't stay up here too long. Alright?"

"You got it." Garret watched the security guard enter back into the building. He knelt and picked up the bag, then headed over to the edge of the roof. "Now to just make sure I do this right." He reached into the container and removed his supplies. He placed them on the ground beside him.

He placed the small camera and faced it toward the restaurant. "Now for a little juice. Good thing we got that new model that runs on batteries." He ripped open the package and inserted the battery into the back of the small orb. He placed the base on the top of the ledge on the side, laying the directional microphone underneath it. He grabbed the roll of duct tape and secured the two items to the ledge. He stood up with a grunt. "Since the microphone has its own internal battery, that should be it." He picked up the now near empty bag and headed back inside. He descended the stairs and at the bottom came face to face with a tall man in a suit.

"Are you Mr. Garrison?" he asked.

"That's right."

"Then hurry up. I don't have all day." Without further

words he headed back toward the initial waiting area Garret had left.

"I don't have much choice at this point, do I?" Garret asked himself. He followed behind the man and entered the room with the nameplate 'Walker'.

"Take a seat," Walker said, pointing at the seat in front of the desk. "Now what are you here for today?" He looked down at the desk as he spoke. He straightened, shuffling some papers. "Judging from your attire, I can hazard a guess."

"Okay, I'll bite. Why do you think I'm here, Mr. Ivy League?" Garret kicked back in the chair and raised his feet to place his heels on the desk with a smirk plastered on his face.

Walker's eyebrows shot up and his face flushed. "Get that foot off my desk right this instant."

"Or what exactly? You going to call for the big boys to take care of your problems like a small child? Or is it you really have no clue who I am?"

Walker gulped and pulled his collar out while looking away. "Forget about that. Fine. Why are you here, sir?"

"I need the best on retainer." Garret removed one foot from the desk and leaned his chair back on two legs. "Word on the street is that would be your law firm. In this line of work," he pointed down at his vest's sergeant at arms tag, "you always need a good lawyer on call, just in case."

"You're aware that would be around four hundred a month, right?"

"Do you think I'm poor or something?" Garret gritted his teeth, removed his foot from the desk, and leaned forward with a scowl. "I can handle that. You worry about this egghead shit you do for a living." His hand snaked around his back and retrieved his wallet. He drew out a handful of bills. He threw them onto the desk. "There, consider that the first payment. Do we have a deal?"

"Just let me draw up some paperwork first, and we can make this official. Please wait here a moment, sir." He ducked out of the room and rapid footsteps could be heard fading away.

"And that's the sign for me to make my exit." He grabbed the bills, stuffed them into his pocket, and exited. He hurried toward the stairwell and ducked inside. He descended the flights and came out on the bottom floor.

"Did everything go well, Mr. Garrison?" the receptionist asked as he emerged from the darkened stairwell.

Garret walked up to the circular desk. "We couldn't see eye to eye." He leaned in and whispered. "He's a bit of a dick, you know."

She brought a hand up to her mouth and stifled a giggle. "You don't have to tell me. He's the one who interviewed me for this position. I'm pretty sure that he kept trying to sneak glances up my skirt."

"What a tasteless thing to do." He affixed a charming smile to his face. "Especially when you're so helpful to the customers."

"I just do my best."

"Yes, I can tell. Don't lose that spark of good in you working here." He pushed off the counter. "I'll see you around."

"Wait a minute." She scribbled down on a nearby notepad. "Here, take this." She ripped out a page and handed it over. "It's for another lawyer around town I know personally. He's a nice guy, talented, and doesn't bullshit you."

Garret took the paper and winked at her. "Thanks, darling. I'll remember this. I owe you one, and I always pay back my debts. Unfortunately, I have to go now. Duty calls. You know how it is." He gave a small wave and turned to exit. He pushed through the clear glass doors and broke into a jog toward the van. He opened the door and climbed inside. He looked to his right. "Is everything setup?"

"I just barely managed to get the feed live. It should be good. We'll get the prospects to watch this all night and see what they see. What took you so long anyway? Did you have any trouble getting to the roof?

"It's a long story."

"Check it out." Skuz pointed across Garret's front when a knock on the window interrupted him.

"Excuse me, sir. You forgot this." The receptionist handed another piece of paper, this one folded up. "My name is Donna by the way."

"Thank you, Donna." Garret flashed a toothy smile.

"See you later, Mr. Garrison." She turned and sashayed back into the office.

Garret unfolded the paper and read the numbers lining the inside.

"Give me that." Skuz ripped the note away. "Dude, you were hitting on her when you're with that scary ogre? You've got some balls alright."

Garret turned the key in the ignition. "Just shut up and worry about your own shit. Alright?"

4

Garret pushed the clubhouse door open. "Where's Rich?"

Tony looked up from his game of solitaire at one of the nearby tables. "He's on the phone in the back bedroom. I'd wait a few minutes if I were you."

"Who's he talking to?" Skuz slammed the door shut. "The cartel?"

"You got me, brother." Tony shrugged, reached up, removed his beanie, and scratched his shaved head before putting the headwear back on. "He didn't seem too happy with how it was going the last I heard."

A loud crash from down the hallway leading to the bedroom interrupted them along with Richard's irate voice. "What the hell are you talking about? You're not serious." The door flung open to reveal Richard pacing in front of the doorway with the phone resting against his shoulder. "We'll see about that." He ripped the device away from his ear and stomped down the hallway toward the group. "How much of that did you hear?"

"From them not being serious. Who are they, and what were they not serious about?"

Richard yanked a seat out and sat beside Tony. "That was Yeltzin. He's getting nervous with all the shit going down lately. He wants to quit. We cannot let that happen."

"Damned right. We pay him well enough," Garret said. "A little risk is in the job description of a meth cooker. We just need to convince him to do the smart thing."

"He always has been a little antsy. It's not surprising he's acting up now of all times," Skuz said. "Should we use honey or vinegar here?"

"Definitely vinegar," Richard said. "He has no leverage, and he knows it. He's only in this country through our good will. He knows better than to piss on our shoes and think he'll get away with it. He was probably using a little of his own supply on the phone to talk to me like that."

"That'll be dangerous," Garret said. "A tweaked-out meth head who's paranoid is not going to take kindly to any of us striding up to his home."

"He knows better than to raise his hand to us."

"When he's sober, sure." Garret looked between the men. "But when his heads warped with that stuff? I'm not so sure."

"He lives in a trailer," Richard growled through his teeth. "It's not like we can come up with any grand plan to sneak in this time. Our options are limited here. What's your suggestion? We absolutely cannot lose his production in this war. It's not an option."

"If financial incentives no longer work, then we move to more effective options." Garret locked eyes with Richard. "You get me?"

"You mean his family?"

"He's doing this to support them while they live free,

right? Explain how they could technically be deported if we made one phone call."

"That's playing with fire, brother," Tony said. "He could fly into a rage if he's on the junk already."

"It's that or let him go, and our meth production as a result. Is that any better? Then we're all as good as dead."

"That's not a two-man job. Garret, you'll be leading our negotiation team tonight."

"Tonight?"

"We're not wasting any time with this. We need to nip this in the bud. Decide how many you need and who you're taking. Just convince him to continue with his chosen career path, that's all."

"If I'm doing this tonight, I'll need Skuz and Tony here at least. Anyone have any ideas how we're going to convince a tweaker to listen to reason?"

"There's always force," Tony shrugged. "Of course, that only works if the cudgel you threaten actually exists."

"Meaning we'd actually have to be in a position to do something to his wife and kid," Garret finished. "Do we know where they are right now?"

"They should be at their apartment across town at this hour." Skuz pulled out his phone and looked at the time. "Why? Are you thinking we should pay them a visit?"

"Not us." Garret smiled and glanced at Richard.

"Me?" Richard's eyebrows raised. "Why?"

"You're the boss. Besides, we don't need you to go all doom and gloom with them. All we need is for you to be there, and then we can use that as leverage when we're at Yeltzin's trailer. Just be nice, and they won't suspect that they're being used as leverage."

Richard tapped the table before nodding. "I like it.

Lucien and I will go and pay a nice visit. Maybe we'll even bring a gift to prove our good will."

"It's settled. We use the family as leverage then?"

"We still officially need a vote." Richard scanned the room. He cupped a hand around his mouth and shouted. "Vote, now! Get your asses out here."

No sound of doors opening or any sign of acknowledgement met their ears. "Where the hell are they?" Garret asked, leaning back in his chair.

"Let me find out." Skuz pulled out his phone and dialed a number. "Yo, where are you two? We have a vote due, like now."

"We're on our way," Lucien's gruff voice replied. "We were just at Irv's physical therapy. Don't get your panties in a twist."

"Just hurry up, old man. You've got an important job tonight."

"I hear that. Count me as a yes. See you boys soon."

"I guess that's our cue to get going then. He said yes, which gives us a majority. Just give us a call when you're in position," Garret said

"I'm ready to go." Tony stood up from the table, his chair screeching as it slid back across the tile. "I've been cooped up here too long today. I need some fresh air, or I'll go nuts."

"You know I'm in to go." Skuz poked a thumb into his own chest. "Who else will keep you out of trouble?"

"Don't go in early," Richard said, pointing at Garret. "Until we're in the family's house you have no leverage, and who knows what a pissed off tweaker will do. It won't be pretty."

"I've got it already. Hell, I'm more worried about what he'll do when he finds out you're at his family's place."

"He'll do nothing," Tony said, smirking. "If he has any sense, he'll capitulate and do whatever we want."

"It feels dirty, but business is business after all," Garret said.

Richard sighed. "I'll have to get a gift before I go. I can't show up empty handed after all. What kind of guest would we be then?"

"You're so full of it," Garret said as the rest stifled a chuckle. "We'll head out then. Is he still living out in the middle of the boondocks?"

"So far as I know. He's probably paranoid about buying anything too lavish for fear of the tax man investigating. You'll know it when you see it by the numerous tire fences, scattered trash, and the shed out back that looks like a stiff wind will knock it down."

"It's only seven. We'll head out now and be back in time to go to sleep at a decent hour for once."

"Get going already, you bums. I'll just get one of the prospects to get me a gift or something while I'm waiting for Lucien to get back."

"Let's go, guys." Garret and Tony followed Skuz's lead and stood up. They headed for the door and pushed it open. "We're taking the van today. If he hears the bikes, shit will head south in a hurry."

"Good idea." Skuz followed the two out and shut the door behind them.

Richard's eyes followed the group out and then snapped to his left after the door shut. He raised his voice. "Prospects, get in here now."

Corey appeared from the storage closet in the back, while Harold and Ronald hurried out of the bedroom across the hallway."

"What the hell were you two doing in there?" Richard

asked Harold and Ronald. "Getting more acquainted with each other?"

Harold cleared his throat. "We were cleaning the room as instructed, sir."

"Yeah, I bet you were."

"It's true, Pres." Corey sat down in the chair.

"Regardless, who feels like going out and getting a gift for me before Lucien and Irving get back here?" He pointed at Harold. "How about you, big man?"

"Of course, sir. What shall I go get?"

"A tasteful gift for a married woman. I don't know, a food item."

"What about a pie?"

"Yeah, just go to a bakery and get an apple pie or something. You can do that, right?"

Harold's feet snapped together. "Yes, sir."

"This isn't basic training. No need to snap to attention, grunt. A simple yes or no works just as well," Richard sneered.

"Sorry, boss."

Richard glared at Harold. "Was I unclear?"

Corey reached up and pushed Harold away. "He said now, you idiot. Get going and hurry up already. Stop wasting time."

Harold immediately sprinted for the door.

"Should I go tell him I think he forgot his keys?" Ronald asked.

"Someone probably should," Corey said. "It may as well be you." He shooed him away.

Ronald jogged to the bar and reached into the shallow, clean ashtray full of keys. He lifted the appropriate key and hurried after the larger man.

"These kids are going to kill me one day." Richard slid down in his chair with an exhale.

Outside Yeltzin's place a while later...

"I have a bad feeling about this." Tony clicked his tongue. "I hate meth heads. They're unpredictable, never mind if their family is threatened."

"It's three versus one. He's not stupid enough to try anything drastic," Skuz said.

"I'm with Tony on this one," Garret said. "Drug addled idiots are hard to deal with, especially those hopped up on crystal. Paranoia sets in, stupid ideas no longer feel so dumb, and you get brave. Too brave for your own good. Still," he blew smoke to his right out the window. "it's something we have to do for the club. There's no way out of it."

"Why aren't his lights on?" Skuz asked. "It's dark. His truck's still here, but there are no lights on."

"Maybe he's out back in the shed right now? I know he's not sleeping this early, unless he's crashing from a meth binge."

"Those can go days. It's more likely we'll catch him in the middle of a manic fit than him sleeping." Tony readjusted himself in his seat.

Garret felt a rumbling in his pants pocket. He kept his eyes on the trailer across the highway as he answered the phone. "Are you in position?"

"We just pulled up now. We'll be ringing the doorbell inside of a minute. Give us five minutes. If you haven't heard back, it's clear. We'll call if we're turned away."

"Got it." Garret hung up. "They're there. Now we just wait and see if they let them in first."

"Hey, just asking out of curiosity's sake, but is it true what they say about firing guns off near a meth lab? That it'll result in an explosion?"

"I don't know, and I don't want to find out. Please try to refrain from shooting anyone tonight," Tony said. His arm snaked around to his lower back. "I really don't want to go burying someone else tonight."

"We're not killing him, dumbass." Garret turned around in his seat and reached back to punch Skuz's leg. "We need him alive and working for us. We need that meth for our deal. It's not negotiable. If we lose him, we need another cooker quick."

"Fine." Skuz rubbed his knee where it was struck. "I'm just not planning to die tonight. If it's him or one of us, he's going down."

"That goes without saying." Garret looked down at his now illuminated phone screen. It only showed two words. "We're in."

"That's our cue, men." Garret shoved the phone down his pants pocket. "Ready?"

"As close as can be expected when we're going to strong-arm a druggie outlaw." Skuz ejected the magazine of his current handgun and reinserted it in the bottom. "I'm good."

"Then let's go." Garret stepped out of the van, looked left and right down the dark highway, and took off in a run across the road. He sauntered forward up the dirt path toward the small trailer. Assorted items were scattered across the front yard, ranging from a toilet, assorted children's toys, and even a few recliners.

"What a dump," Skuz muttered beside Garret. "You'd have to be nuts to let it get this bad."

"Or a stereotypical redneck."

"Why not paint yourself as an uneducated simpleton in the eyes of the law when you're really a master chemist?" Garret asked. "It's actually ingenious." He looked to his left, poked Tony's shoulder, and pointed to the left. "Go around and cover the back in case he runs. And be careful."

"I'm with you," Skuz said, standing to the right of the door, out of sight to anyone inside.

Garret stepped up to the screen door and knocked. A male voice grunted and called back. "Get out of here. I'm in no mood to deal with delinquents at this hour."

The inside door swung open to reveal a disheveled man with an out-of-control beard taking over his face. He reached up and scratched the mess of hair. "Oh, it's you. What do you want? Let me guess. It's about the cooking?"

"Come on, Yeltz. You know how this works. I don't want to be here, and that goes double for you. Rich sent me over to smooth this out."

Yeltzin grunted and his eyes narrowed. "There's nothing to work out. I'm done with this shit."

"I was afraid you'd say that. We're prepared for that attitude. I really wish you hadn't forced us on this though."

"What are you saying?" Yeltzin took a step back and bared his teeth. "What have you done?"

"Go ahead, call your wife. Find out, if you're so curious. Just know you have three gunmen trained on your ass at all times, so don't try anything stupid."

He flipped on a dim light inside and moved to the nearby phone. He kept his eyes locked on Garret as he dialed the number. "Elvira, is anything happening right now?"

"Yeltzin? I told you to stop calling here. I was just hosting a little impromptu get together with Rich and Lucien. Can you believe it? It's been years."

One of his hands fell to his side and shook. He never lost sight of Garret's grinning face. "Is everything going okay, dear? They're not trying anything?"

"You must be strung out again. No, you paranoid meth-head. They're doing nothing wrong, except not bringing ice cream to go with the pie." She laughed and numerous voices could be heard joining her in a chorus on the other end. "Oh, here, Rich wants to talk. Don't call here anymore. I mean it this time."

"Wait a minute."

Richard's voice greeted him. "Sorry, Yeltz. We just wanted to drop by and check in. You know how it is. We had to see if everything's still in order here. Which, by the way, it is. Your ex-wife is a hell of an interior decorator. Your daughter is adorable, by the way. She's got everything under control from what I see here. It's been nice talking to you again, buddy. Now I'd listen to Garret if I were you. Bye."

Yeltzin slammed the earpiece back onto the receiver with a yell before turning back to Garret. "You son of a whore. You'd dare bring them into this?"

"You got them into this. Blame yourself, or God. I don't much care which. The fact is, you're not quitting. If you go all psycho on us, so will Rich. We've got you by the balls here. Just do the smart thing. You're surrounded anyway. You stand no chance."

"You wouldn't dare kill my baby."

"I notice there was no mention of Elvira there. Go ahead, test us. You think we haven't had to do some heinous shit before in this life? You'll be gambling with their lives. But let me ask this. Do you feel lucky?" He threw on his biggest shit eating grin.

"If I help you, the cartel will just do the same thing to them. You can't protect them from those animals. Not that you're much better."

"We're at war with them. The only reason we're pushing so hard is that we need your product in our battle. So, help us fight them, or make enemies of both groups. Which sounds smarter?"

Skuz stepped out from the side and stood by Garret. "The answer's obvious." He raised his voice. "Hey, Tony. How's the view from that side?"

"I can see the back of his head just fine. Just give me a reason."

"It seems I don't have much of a choice, do I?" Yeltzin asked. "Fine, I'll keep working. But if anything happens to them, I will turn into your worst nightmare. I won't care what happens to me."

"Yeah, whatever. When will the next batch be done if we get you your medicine?"

"After I receive the cold medicine, it'll take a few days. That's always the limiting factor."

"You're in luck." Skuz reached inside his jacket and threw down a multicolored box. "Here you go."

"Where did you get that?" Garret asked

"That one dude's bathroom."

"I should have known," Garret sighed. "Anyway, do we have a deal?" He reached his hand out in front of him.

Yeltzin glared down at the palm and hissed. "Yeah, for now. But mark my words, this isn't over."

"Yeah, whatever," Garret smirked as the door was slammed in his face. He raised his voice to be heard from all over the property. "Let's head back home then. Our work's done."

5

"I wish I could have been there and seen his face when I hung up." Richard downed the mug of coffee sitting in front of him. "His wife was sure accommodating though."

"Tell me you didn't." Garret sat beside him.

"He didn't what?" Ann asked from the bar. She poured another cup of coffee and hauled it over. She placed it down in front of Garret and stayed there. "Don't give me that club business bullshit."

"We were just convincing an asset to keep producing is all," Richard said. "He's the stubborn type, so we had to get creative."

"It all worked out in the end," Garret said, pulling out a seat beside him. "Take a load off those pretty legs, won't you? Let the prospects take care of that stuff."

"Ronald," Ann called out.

Ronald's stocky form approached the table. "Yes?"

"Would you be a dear and take over the bar duties for a few minutes, please?"

"Yes, ma'am." Ronald scurried off behind the bar.

"Everything worked out then?" she asked. "Is that why you were so late coming home yesterday?"

"You got it. We're set for the future though. We got our cold medicine connection, and now we have our cooker." Garret stopped and looked over at Richard. "Now we only have to worry about the damned cartel."

A buzzing sound interrupted the group. Richard took out his phone and smiled. "We have company. Corey's letting him in right now. He says he has something urgent to speak about."

"If it isn't one thing it's another," Garret said.

The door to the club swung open. Kelly made a bee line over to the table. "You gents mind if I take a seat?"

"By all means." Richard gestured to the chair. "What brings you over here this morning?"

"You haven't heard? It's all over the streets."

"Apparently not," Garret said. "Spill it."

"I think it's better if you see this yourself." Kelly got up and walked over to the television perched above them in the corner of the room. He grabbed the nearby remote and turned it on. He switched channels to a news station and turned the volume up.

"Police say a Ms. Elvira Yeltzin was found dead this morning, along with her daughter. Sources say there may be signs of breaking and entering, and incredible force was used in the act."

"Christ," Ann said. "Isn't that where you went last night?"

Kelly walked back to the table and tossed the remote control down on the table. "I assume this wasn't you boys?"

"Hell no," Richard said. "We paid them a visit last night on unrelated business. This has to be them." He gritted his teeth. "They followed us last night. They're going after our infrastructure. They're smart."

"This is going to fuck everything up," Garret said. "Yeltzin's going to be on the war path now. As if we didn't have enough enemies. We also need to replace him."

"What did he do? I may be able to help with personnel," Kelly said.

"He was our cooker. He was hesitant to keep working for us, so we paid him and his wife a visit last night."

"They followed you to set an example. It sounds like they don't want anyone to work with you. Classic tactics, divide and conquer. Still, we don't have a cooker. If we did, we wouldn't need you blokes to supply us. I hope you find a new one soon, because we need that crystal to finance our operation too."

"We get that," Richard growled. "We only have one other cooker on our roster, and she's a little kooky, but we don't have a choice now."

"I'd hoped we wouldn't have to involve her." Garret shook his head. "We also need to keep an eye on Yeltzin. He'll be out for blood after last night."

"We'll take care of him tonight after dark. He's out in the middle of nowhere. Nobody will miss him."

"Take who you need, and don't take any chances. Bring a rifle and take him out from a distance. We can't risk anything else. Take care of him afterward."

"I'd love to volunteer, gentlemen, but I have a job I need to get back to myself. I was just sent over here to make sure you're aware of last night, and to see if you had a plan to deal with the fallout. I'm pleased with what I see here. I'll report just that. Just don't make this a habit."

"We won't," Richard said. "Now be careful on your way

back." He stood up and hugged Kelly before taking a step back. "Should I send an escort with you to be sure?"

"I appreciate that, Rich, but I'm cool. It sounds like you men need all your resources here. "Oh," his right hand dug into his pants pocket, "I almost forgot." He pulled out a cell phone and placed it on the table. "Use this for calling us. Just for safety's sake you understand."

"Right," Richard said. "If you need anything, don't hesitate to call on us."

"We've got your back," Garret said.

"That's good, because we have a hint on where those blokes are hiding out. We'll need some help when we go after them."

"You can count on us," Richard said.

"It'll be soon, but we're not sure when. We heard it was near a restaurant."

"We already have eyes and ears on it. Harold should be watching them as we speak."

"How the hell did you manage that?" Kelly asked.

"I'm good at being subtle," Garret said.

"When you get any real intel out of your subtlety, let us know. For now, I'm out, gents. Best of luck today." Kelly walked away and out the door.

"Don't you two need a vote for this?" Ann asked the two men. "You know, for taking out Yeltzin?"

"She's right," Garret said. "We have two yea votes, but we need to call a meeting before I head out. Let me go check Skuz's vote. He should be in the back. You call Tony and get his vote. I have a feeling it will be yes."

"I hate doing that over the phone," Richard said. "Fine, I'll go get my burner." He got up from the table and went over to the box near the bar.

Ann got up and followed Garret to the storage room

door. "I'm going with you tonight. Don't even try stopping me. I don't want a repeat of last night. I'll watch for tails."

"I know better than to argue with you." Garret knocked on the door. "Yo, we've got a vote. Stop getting the prospect to blow you and get out here already."

The door opened. Skuz pointed up to the top shelf. "Get it up there already. All this better be filed away before I get back."

"I thought that was Irving's job," Ann commented.

"He went home early tonight. I took it on myself to finish his job. Someone needs to help him out besides the old man. He's been running himself ragged since Irv got himself shot."

"I wouldn't let him hear you say that," Garret said, leading the group to the table where he'd left Rich. "What's the word?"

"Tony says yes, along with Lucien." He folded the phone up and put it on the table. He looked up at Skuz. "What about you? Do you agree we should deal with Yeltzin before he gets even with us?"

"Damned skippy. You know I'm in." He punched his right hand into his open left palm. "That dude's always pissed me off."

"That's five. The vote passes." Richard smiled. "Now take who you need while I go sit in a dark room with Harold staring at a screen. I can't trust that entirely to a prospect after all. If we're lucky, by the time you get back we should have an idea of how we're going to tackle it. At the very least we'll know when to strike."

"Sounds good." Garret extended his arm and poked Skuz in the chest. "You're with me, chucklehead. Bring a prospect with us. Without Tony we're short on manpower."

"Where the hell's he at anyway?" Skuz asked.

"He had to go visit his sister I think," Richard said.

"We got us a group then. I'll take the place of the prospect," Ann said, leaning against Garret's side. "I'll handle the driving, and you two get the muscle work. That is what you wanted, right big boys?"

"Somehow that pisses me off, but fine. That will work fine," Garret said.

"Good, because I don't want to have to carry that piece of crap."

"I knew you really were weak," Skuz said, a smug grin plastered on his face. "Just let us guys lift it, sweet cakes. We've got it."

"Take your dick waving contest out to that trailer and get it done then," Richard laughed. "But be careful. He's likely to be armed. I'd even carry a weapon if I were you, Ann. He's not likely to be lenient just because you lack a 'y' chromosome."

"How nice of you to worry about little old me." She brought a hand to her chest and curtsied in front of Richard. "I almost miss the days when you'd shoo me away and tell me it was none of my business."

"And now I remember why I did that. Go on. Get out of here already."

"Be back later, Pres." Garret led the group out of the building and into the parking lot outside. He took off his vest. He jogged into the garage and came back empty handed. "Let's get ready." He punched Skuz in the shoulder, shaking him back to attention. "Take off your kutte. We're going in the van."

"It feels like we spend more time in the fricking van than we do on our bikes."

"You know the drill. We can't be wearing our colors or

representing the club when performing overt illegal activities. Deal with it."

"Yeah, yeah." Skuz took off the vest and tossed it on a nearby chair inside the garage. "Do we have a plan by the way, or are we just rolling up and blasting the place?"

"Getting into a prolonged gun fight with a meth head isn't a great plan," Ann said.

"We're doing what Rich suggested. We're getting a rifle and blowing his head off in one shot. He won't even know we're there. We'll stop by my place, pick it up, and assemble it on site. As soon as we fire, we peel out. Simple enough, right?"

"Just make sure you don't miss, hot shot," Ann said. "Which of you is the better shot? Because if the morning toilet is anything to go by, it's not you, dear."

"Wait, what now?" Skuz asked.

"Never mind her. I'll take the shot." Garret's face glowed a brilliant red and gave a brief glare toward Ann.

"If you say so. Just don't miss this time. I'm tired of cleaning up after you." She opened the driver's door and climbed inside. "Hurry up. Let's get this over with. I assume you have a plan for where to take the remains afterward?"

"Always," Garret said. He glared daggers toward Skuz who was failing to disguise his laughter. Without further words, Garret got inside the van and called out the window. "Hurry up."

"Right away, deadeye." Skuz snickered and threw open the back doors. He shut them behind him, and the van lurched forward.

Near Yeltzin's trailer...

Ann pumped the brake and came to a stop. She pointed ahead. "You've got a little hike ahead of you, but this is as close as I can comfortably get without him seeing us. Stay low, and don't miss. I'll drive up after I hear the shot. Jump in, and we're gone. How's that for a plan?"

"Works for me," Skuz said. "All I have to do is watch your back while you two do all the work."

"I think we may have a bigger problem than that." The van moved again. Ann pulled the van behind a thicket of trees on the nearby dirt trail leading off the road.

"What's up?" Skuz smushed his face against the window and saw a lone police cruiser sitting outside the trailer. "Shit. What are they doing here?"

"They probably suspect him of killing his family, or they're trying to protect him from whoever killed them," Ann said. "Which means this just got ten times harder. We'll need to get rid of them first before we do anything."

"How are we going to do that?" Skuz asked.

"Give them a good reason to have somewhere else to be. I can think of at least two ideas off the top of my head." Garret stared out the side window at the car. "One would require an emergency call in and the report of a crime near enough to here so that they'd be the ones assigned."

"What's the second?"

"The second involves ignoring him and getting creative with this van."

"I don't like the sound of that one," Ann said. "The first plan is safer. I vote for it."

"Well, let's at least hear the second plan," Skuz said. "It might actually be better than falsely reporting a crime on a cell phone that could feasibly be traced."

"Shit. When you put it like that, go ahead," Ann said.

"Okay, so you know how the only way people can find

snipers is by the sound, right? I heard a lot of snipers like to post up like ten feet from a window in a room to obfuscate their sound. No one can tell where the crack came from because it's muffled in the room, right?"

"You're not saying we shoot out the back of the van, are you?"

"Why not?" Garret asked. "We'd be able to make our escape in no time, it'd be inconspicuous, and the sound wouldn't be nearly so loud. All we'd do is angle this van so that the back faces the trailer, crack the door, and we're in business."

"If you absolutely must do it that way, I recommend calling and getting him to move first. Combining the two plans would make more sense." She raised a hand in the darkness, revealing a lit up rectangle. "I'm more than willing to make the call myself before I reposition."

"Go for it," Garret said. "Just don't make it too close. We don't want more units coming here."

"I know the perfect place." Ann's long fingers dialed the three numbers and raised the phone to her ear. Her voice turned quivering and quiet. "Hello? Police? Oh my God, there's a crazy man firing off shots around the local high school. Yes, I still hear them cracking off. Please send someone now. Someone could be hurt. Oh my God, I have to go and hide." She ended the phone call. "Now we watch and see."

Skuz kept his eyes glued to the car. "He's beginning to move."

"Of course he is. The high school is near here. He'd be the one they'd call. Which means we have a limited time window to get this done now." She turned the key in the ignition after she saw the cruiser pull off onto the road. She flipped the car around. "How's that?"

"Perfect." Garret laid down on his stomach on the floor. He looked over to Skuz. "Crack the door open and see if there's a strong wind.

Skuz pushed the door open until he heard Garret stop him. "None at all."

"That's good enough. I have a clear sight of the entire trailer from here. Now where is that son of a bitch?" He pressed his eye up against the scope and peered through it. "I found him. He's near his bed. Prepare to get us out of here." He inhaled, and his right index finger wrapped around the trigger.

"Wait." Skuz patted Garret on the back.

"What now?" Garret growled through his teeth. "I have the shot."

"There's a car coming. Wait for it to pass. It'll give the perfect cover. People will just think it's a backfire if they hear anything and actually bother to look," Skuz said. He watched the random car pass by. "Now you're clear."

"Finally." Garret centered the cross hairs over his target and lifted them a few inches. "That should do it for this distance. Bye, Yeltz." His finger squeezed, and the target in his sites fell. A mist of blood caked the trailer's glass windows. Garret pulled back on the slide, and a cartridge fired out. He sat up and looked out the back. "Got him. Let's go!"

Skuz pulled the back door shut and laughed. "That was awesome. You hit him right in the head it looked like. That'll be a closed casket funeral for sure."

"More than likely. I'd be surprised if he still has a head anymore after that." Garret disassembled the rifle and packed it away in the nearby box he'd brought. He picked up the lone cartridge that bounced out of the rifle and tossed it in the box.

The van rolled over a few bumps on the way toward the road. "Yeah, it looked like a clean shot from here, but who knows?" Ann said. Her face lost all color. "Oh, fuck me. We have a huge problem." She pulled to the side of the road as a caravan of police cars zoomed past them. She hopped into the back and pushed Skuz to the front. "You're sitting in the driver's seat now. Don't drive off until it's clear."

"What the hell?" Skuz stumbled into the driver's seat and looked forward. "Oh crap."

"Exactly. Follow my lead if you two want to stay free through the night."

"One of them is coming over here."

"Let him." Ann slid the box behind her, pushed Garret down on top of the rifle's case, and pounced on top of Garret. "Now follow my lead." She leaned down and captured his lips with her own.

"Is that really the best time for this?" Skuz asked. He looked back toward the road and saw one officer drawing close. He rolled down the window. "Yes, Officer?"

"What are you doing here on the side of the road at this hour?"

"It's my clients' idea, not mine." Skuz pointed over his shoulder.

The officer stuck his head inside the window and looked behind Skuz. "Oh for God's sake, you three. You're lucky I don't slap an indecent exposure charge on you for this. Lucky for you, I have bigger fish to fry. Now you two, go find a motel or something. Get out of here. There's a shooter around."

"Holy shit. Seriously?" Skuz's eyes bugged out. "We'll leave immediately, Officer. Thanks for the warning."

"Just get out of here, you stupid kids." The older officer shook his graying head.

"And you," the police officer poked Skuz's chest, "try to find a better career than driving around horny people for God's sake, boy."

"We all have our problems, Officer. It's not like I enjoy the job. We've all got to make money however we can."

"Yeah, well get out of here. It's not safe around here at this time of night."

"Will do," Skuz nodded. "Have a nice night."

The officer grumbled as he turned away and trudged back to his cop car.

Ann climbed off Garret and wiped her mouth. "The key to police interaction is making them not want to be there anymore. That's all. Aren't you glad you brought me along?"

"We'd be screwed without you, sweetie." Garret climbed off the floor and cradled his lower back.

"Damned straight you would." She glanced back up front. "Hurry up and get going, pervert. The show's over. Besides, the cop's waiting on you to move."

"I never knew you wanted a career as a taxi driver, buddy. That was some quick thinking."

Skuz pulled out onto the road. "She said play along, so I did."

"You do have some use after all, instead of just getting yourself into trouble," Ann said smiling. "You should listen more often."

"Let's just get back before anything else happens tonight," Skuz said, watching the line of police cruisers blast past him in the opposite lane.

Garret watched the line of cars whiz past. "At least we'll get some sleep, unlike those poor bastards."

"I thought it was supposed to be 'No rest for the wicked', not the opposite," Ann quipped.

"Rest?" Garret let out a laugh. "You must be new to this life."

Ann frowned and elbowed Garret in the ribs. "You need to read the mood more."

"My bad."

6

"At least that's one less thing to worry about." Richard flicked off the television. He saw Skuz, Garret, and Ann enter the clubhouse. "Your exploits are on the news. Not very quiet, but effective. They have no idea where the shot even came from, much less who did it."

"Weren't you supposed to be watching the webcam I set up with Harold?" Garret asked.

"We found plenty." Richard rubbed the sides of his head. "He's still in there, but my eyes were starting to hurt so I took a break. Executive privilege and all."

"What'd we find?" Garret pulled out a chair for Ann and then one for himself. He sat down. "Anybody noteworthy going in and out?"

"As a matter of fact, yeah. You could say that." A smug grin appeared on Richard's face. "It wasn't easy to confirm it, but we saw a higher up shot caller in ES-15 going in three times a day on the dot. He never goes in earlier or later. He goes in at ten am, two pm, and finally again at 9 pm after they close."

"Probably getting their cut," Skuz said. "He wouldn't

want to risk someone else getting that money. The last time someone appeared incompetent it didn't end well for them in that group."

"I can personally attest to that," Richard said. "Anybody seeing the same opportunity I am?"

"We're going after that money?" Garret asked. "How in the world would we pull that off in the middle of the day while all those people are there?"

"I didn't say we'd go in during the day," Richard said.

"Nighttime breaking and entering?" Ann asked. "I don't know about that. Statistically speaking, those don't work so well. That's what everyone's alarm systems are designed against."

"Nah," Richard said, "nothing so dramatic. This could be accomplished as a plain clothes operation by someone with fast hands and a little distraction."

"What do you have in mind?" Garret asked.

"We have a few options - either steal the money or take the direct route."

"You're suggesting kidnapping the cartel shot caller?" Skuz asked. "I'm up for that. Extract some information from him, and we'll be in business."

"They'll notice either way," Garret said. "Which would be more effective? Sewing dissention in their ranks or gaining valuable intel?"

"Assuming we can get the guy to talk," Ann said. "These cartel types are real OG's. They'll never rat."

"You leave that to your boyfriend. I have faith that he could loosen his tongue if it comes to that," Skuz said.

"Call a meet," Richard said. "We need to talk this one over before we make any decisions. As soon as everyone's here, the meeting starts. Don't be late. I'll let Lucien know." He pulled out a phone and started punching in numbers.

"I got Tony." Garret followed suit.

"Get over here as soon as possible and grab Irving while you're at it. We have urgent business to discuss," Richard said. "Good. See you soon." He hung up. "Irving and Lucien are on their way."

"So is Tony. He just visited his sister again," Garret said.

"Then we'll have our meeting, and we can finally get some shut eye tonight." Richard rubbed his blood shot eyes. "I'm getting too old for this job."

"Then I'll go make some instant coffee. You'll need to be awake for this." Ann got up and meandered over to the bar.

"You know," Richard said watching Ann walk away, "even though she's a giant pain in the ass, she's a good old lady."

"When she wants to be," Garret said.

"Trouble in paradise?" Skuz asked.

"No, it's nothing. It's probably just my imagination," Garret said.

"You probably just need to spend more time with her," Richard said. "In my experience, women tend to get pissy when you ignore them for your job." He glanced back at Garret. "Sound familiar?" he asked with a smirk.

"Well, when you put it like that..." Garret trailed off.

"You never were good at keeping girlfriends, as I recall from high school," Skuz said. "You used to go through them at a pace of one a month." He counted on his fingers. "You had to have had at least twelve throughout senior year."

"Maybe we should focus more on the job at hand instead of my personal matters?" Garret asked, looking away from the group.

"Fair enough," Richard said. "Besides my right hand's questionable taste in women, which are you guys leaning on the vote?"

Skuz scratched the sides of his shaved head and then fiddled with the dyed purple hair on the top of his head. "Personally? I'd go with the money plan. What's better than shifting the blame onto someone else?"

"That's only if it goes off without a hitch," Richard said. "If it doesn't, we're in the same shit as the other plan."

"Minus the valuable intel that one of their shot callers could give us," Garret said. "I lean toward kidnapping the OG. I can get him to talk. Combine that with the Outback Boys, and we have the makings of a solid assault in the making. Maybe strong enough to push them back over the border if we're lucky. One of those 'make it untenable to remain up here' things."

Lucien and Irving pushed the nearby door open. Lucien grunted. "You know how I hate calling meets over the phone this late."

"You hate proxy votes by phone more," Richard said. "It's mandatory this happens tonight, old man. You'll understand once we explain." Richard looked over at Irving. "What about you, Irv? Are you up for a little late-night strategizing?"

Irving hopped away from Lucien's shoulder and took a seat at the table. "Anytime, anywhere."

"That's what I like to hear," Richard said. He looked up at Lucien. "Where did that attitude go?"

"It disappeared into a vapor in my late fifties. Still, where's Tony?" Lucien scanned the room. "All I see is the prospects cleaning up."

"He's on his way," Skuz said. "He should be here soon. When he gets here, we can start."

"Sorry I'm late." Tony shut the door behind him. "What are we voting on?"

Everybody at the table, minus Irving, stood up. Richard

spoke up. "Let's get in the room and get this started. The sooner we do, the sooner we can sleep tonight."

Garret and Skuz helped Irving out of his chair as the older members filed in ahead. They slammed the door shut behind them and took their places at the table.

"Alright, we have a few options ahead of us." Richard clasped his hands and laid them on the wooden table in front of him. "We have video evidence that one of their higher up shot callers visits their restaurant three times a day, every day, at the same time. He goes there to pick up a brown bag every few hours. Presumably it's a vig they're kicking up to stay in business."

"What's the play then? Rush in and hold up a busy restaurant in the middle of the day?" Lucien scoffed. "That'll never work in time without the cops showing up."

"That is certainly an option, but not one I was going to suggest," Richard said. "If we were going to steal the money, we'd have to be a bit more subtle than a smash and grab."

"We don't even have to do that in the first place," Garret said. "I prefer the other idea personally. It'd give us more intel and leverage to use."

"What's that?" Lucien asked.

"We know where their lieutenant is three times a day, right?" Garret asked. "Well, what better time is there to kidnap, torture, interrogate, and gain some valuable insight into how they think?"

"Shouldn't we be trying to de-escalate?" Irving asked.

"It's too late for that," Garret said. "Once they start sending attack helicopters after us, that time has passed. All we can do now is win this war. To do that, we need to know how they're thinking. He could tell us where they're positioned, where their safe houses are, and maybe even where the big kahuna is."

"Or go the mosquito route," Lucien said. "If we just take the money, we put him under the limelight and put pressure in the ranks."

"That's basically the picture. Anybody have any thoughts to add?" Richard asked.

"I say we go after the dude," Garret crossed his arms and looked over toward Lucien. "Going after the money is high risk, low reward. At least my way is high risk, high reward. With him, we could learn exactly where to strike to end this beef once and for all."

"Where would we even keep him?" Skuz asked. "We sure as shit couldn't do it here."

"We can always find a place," Garret said. "Out in the middle of the wilderness in the middle of the night would do just fine. It'd also cut down on disposal time, since we could bury him right there."

"I say we take one of them bastards out," Tony said. "If it just so happens to be a shot caller, so be it. I tend to lose my empathy when they send an armored vehicle after us. Considering we'd get a bunch of useful knowledge, it's just a bonus if you ask me."

"We can't let ourselves be blinded with rage," Richard said. "Tell them, Lucien."

Lucien looked down at the table and tapped the wooden surface before looking over at Richard and the rest of the group. "Playing pussy foot isn't going to win this either. They're certainly pulling no punches. I say we don't either. I agree with Garret and Tony on this one, Pres."

"Stealing the money would be the subtle option," Irving said, leaning on an elbow, "But I don't think now is the time for subtle, considering we're in the middle of a war with these savages."

"That's right." Lucien banged on the table which caused everyone to start to chatter at the same time.

Richard pounded the gavel. "Easy."

The group quieted down until Lucien continued. "These assholes wanted a war. I say we give them one. Show them no mercy, and make them look weak. They're already losing ground in Mexico. It's obvious they're trying to project strength up north. If they lose up here, their rivals will swoop in and take care of them below the border."

"Which would cut off any and all reinforcements coming across," Garret said.

"It could also send them into a frothing rage," Irving said. "It could prompt not one, but a whole squadron of attack helicopters next time."

"I have to agree with Irv on this one," Tony said looking down at the table. "I think it'd be better to play this one with a bit more subtlety."

"Man, screw that," Skuz said. "If my boy says he can get the guy to talk, I say we give him the chance to end this war quickly."

Richard looked back and forth between the group before smiling. "Time to put it to a vote then. All in favor of just grabbing the money raise your hands."

Irving and Tony raised their hands.

"All those in favor of kidnapping their shot caller and questioning him, raise your hands." Richard raised his hand and saw Garret, Lucien, and Skuz raise theirs. "The vote's settled. Tomorrow we grab the higher up, question him, and start crafting our final blow after his interrogation. Tomorrow morning we'll come up with the plan." Richard yawned and raised a hand in front of his mouth. "For now, we all need some sleep." He banged the gavel down on the wooden circle in front of him.

"Tomorrow will be interesting for sure." Irving pushed himself up with a grimace. "I'll stay and watch the film myself."

"So you can create us a plan?" Garret asked. "No offense, but I don't think that's your strong point."

"I have to do something, man. I can't sit around all day and accomplish nothing. The least I can do is get on the internet and scour it for the blueprints of the newly created restaurant. It shouldn't be too hard to find if I check the darknet. You can always find whatever you need there, for a price."

"How the hell do you send money without it being traced anyway?" Skuz asked.

"Someone's never heard of crypto currency and mixing I see. The trick is to send it the right way and not leave something to trace back. Meaning, buy the crypto without leaving a paper trail among other things. It's not exactly complicated."

"It sounds like Greek to me," Lucien said. "Whatever, it just means I don't need to drop you off before I head home. Have fun training to be an egghead."

"Teach one of the prospects while you're at it. We need more technologically literate people here," Richard said, standing up. "Besides, you're going to want one of them getting you stuff throughout the night anyway. You may as well teach them something too." He raised his hands above his head, stretched, and a massive yawn escaped his mouth. "I'm heading straight home to bed. I don't know about all of you."

The Next Morning...

"Please tell me I don't need to go buy any more gifts." Ronald tried to catch his breath after barging through the door. He walked over and handed the card to Irving who was sitting at the computer. "Why do you need these again?"

"To send for this information. I have a seller inside the city records office who's willing to part with them for the right price. That's where you come in. These are as good as money, without putting my identity online." He scratched off the codes on the cards and typed them into the website. "Now all I need to do is transfer the funds off the site to my personal paper wallet and send them. We'll have the floor plans within minutes, provided they're online, which it says they are."

"How the hell did you learn this?" Ronald stared slack jawed at the screen. "This is like some hacker stuff right here."

"Not really, man." Irving kept his focus on the monitor as he talked. "It's just basic economics combined with a black market is all. There's a need, and a supply steps up for the right price."

A lighthearted dinging sound interrupted the conversation from the speakers.

"There it is." Irving clicked on the in-site inbox and downloaded the image file. "This is it." He closed the dark web browser and opened the newly received file. A blue mess of lines and assorted floors opened on screen. "This will make today much easier. See now why it was so important?"

"Apparently so," Ronald said. "You need anything else?"

"No, go get some sleep. You deserve it. Before you do, wake up Corey and Harold though. They'll take your place for the day. You get the day off since you stayed up all night. Just be back here tomorrow morning."

"Yes, sir." Ronald stumbled out from the corner of the room. He pulled out his phone and disappeared down the hallway.

"Now to make heads or tails out of this." Irving leaned toward the screen and his eyes narrowed. "I think this is the entrance at least." He tilted his head. "Maybe?" He sighed. "Dammit, I'm too tired for this." He rubbed his eyes and shook his head.

"Morning, ladies." The door pushed open. Garret swaggered in. He approached Irving and stood behind him. "Jackpot." He let his hand fall to Irving's shoulder and patted. "Good job, dude. How did you manage to find that?"

"You just have to know who to ask and who to pay. It's simple enough. Just let me print this out and we can pore over it." He clicked the mouse a few times until a loud buzzing and screeching filled the place. He winced. "We really need a newer printer."

"Then pay for it yourself. This one still works, so good luck getting Rich to buy another one. You know how he is with finances," Garret laughed.

"Help me up, and we can look this over before everyone gets here." Irving reached up and used Garret to steady himself. "Hopefully I'll be able to walk on my own again soon. I'm tired of this shit."

"You got shot twice in a night, buddy. You're fine," Garret said, ripping the paper away from the printer and helping Irving over to a nearby table. He pulled out a chair and helped him sit down. He slammed the paper down and dragged a chair over to sit beside Irving. He jabbed a finger over the blue paper. "Judging from these, I'm guessing this is the front door."

"Morning, ladies." Richard pushed the clubhouse door open and stepped inside. He shuffled over to the table and placed his palms on either side of the blue paper. "Holy shit. Who managed to get this?" He looked up at Garret.

"Don't look at me. This was all Irv here." Garret patted Irving on the shoulder.

"I'll be damned." Richard leaned down and studied the paper. "This is exactly what we needed."

"Yeah, it only cost forty dollars all told."

"Money well spent." Richard pulled up a chair from a nearby table and sat on the other side of Irving. "This looks like where that jackass strode in every single time he visited." Richard brought his index finger down onto the paper. "He went around the back every single time. He parked in the back and walked in without anyone noticing. He slipped out just as easily."

"What are you thinking?" Garret asked.

"I'm thinking we park around here." Richard pointed to a location slightly off the paper. "When we see him pull up, we roll up, grab him, and leave before anyone even knows what just happened."

"You're talking a straight up snatch and run?" Garret asked. "In the middle of broad daylight? On a likely armed target?"

"If you have a better idea, by all means grace us with your intellect," Richard said, a sarcastic tinge lacing his voice.

"My plan requires a bit more time, but it's safer overall. We could still park there behind the place." He traced his finger over to the back of the building. "The difference is, we watch him the first time. We see whether or not he's packing, how long he stays inside, and if he's meeting anyone below board there."

"You mean another ES-15?"

"They're not making three bags of money every day selling burritos, I'll tell you that."

"You're saying there are reinforcements there," Richard said, "which means we'd have to grab him quietly."

"Exactly. My guess is the place is a front. In the front they serve customers. In the back they probably sell all manner of contraband. Drugs, weapons - you name it, they probably sell it back there. Who's going to call the cops on an old Mexican couple in this day and age? No one wants that PR nightmare."

"I never saw anyone out back. If they are in there, they're inside the kitchen or back room."

"Which works to our advantage," Garret said. "After he goes in, we post up outside the door. As soon as he comes out and shuts the door, we grab him. The van drives up, we toss him inside, and we're golden. It'd just require whoever's driving the van to pay attention and go when we signal."

"That sounds an awful lot like Rich's plan, except with a little waiting," Irving said.

"I still say observing them the first pickup would be to our advantage. It gets him relaxed, lazy, and unobservant if he thinks he's safe. I'd be on high alert on the first pickup of the day."

More rumbling outside interrupted the conversation. Moments later the entire group of Lucien, Tony, Skuz, and Ann entered the clubhouse.

"That looks neat." Skuz hurried over and leaned over the table, peering down at the blueprints.

Lucien shoved him aside and pulled up a chair before sitting down. "I assume we'll be beating out a plan, beyond straight kidnapping?"

Ann circled around the table and wrapped her arms around Garrett. "Where did you sneak off to this morning?

You're not trying to leave me out of the fun stuff again, are you?" Her dainty voice betrayed the hidden ferocity boiling beneath. She squeezed. "I know you wouldn't try that again."

"If anything, she'd make this easier," Richard said. "How do you feel about being a distraction for us?"

"Is that all?" Ann stood up straight, and a hand fell to her hips. "That's child's play."

"Then I guess mama bear's distracting him while her boyfriend grabs him. Isn't love wonderful, boys?"

A raucous round of affirmatives and laughter echoed in the room.

"Here's the plan then." Richard leaned forward and clasped his hands in front of him. "Garret, Ann, and Tony will go and pick up our new guest. In the meantime, the rest of us will split up between finding a place to question him in peace and heading over to the Outback Boys' place. They called me earlier. They need a little help it seems. Lucien, you know the quietest places around here. As soon as you have a place, call Garret. Irving and Skuz, you're coming with me. We'll see what they need when we get there. With any luck they'll be interested in aiding in our questioning as well. Any questions?"

"Yeah, I got one." Skuz raised his hands. He paused and looked at everyone before speaking up again. "Did anyone fill up the van yet?"

"We'll have to stop for gas on the way then," Garret said.

"Just checking."

7

"I was wondering when we'd see the big boss man," Kelly said with a shake of Richard's hand.

"We've got something special lined up today and we may need your most persuasive questioner, if you catch my drift."

"Oi, that's me. If you ever need someone to reveal their deepest darkest secrets under penalty of mutilation, I'm your guy."

"I'll remember that for later today if we have problems. Try to be open around mid-day if you can."

"I'll clear up my schedule just in case." Kelly cracked his knuckles. "Anyway, the boss wants to see you boys." He turned around and pointed to the nearby building. "He's waiting inside."

"You two stay here. I'll talk to him myself and see what's up."

"You got it, boss." Skuz nodded.

"Mate," Kelly looked at Irving. "What happened to you?"

"Our newest addition here is battle tested is what happened," Skuz smirked. "He may not look it, but he's a tough son of a bitch. I'd put him up against any of you when he's healed."

"Is that right?" Kelly asked. "No offense, mate, but you don't look like much."

"That's what the other guys thought too," Irving said.

Kelly clapped his hands. "Fair enough."

"Have you heard about what's going on?" Skuz asked.

"It's not my place to say." Kelly looked away and went quiet.

"Oh come on, man," Skuz said. "We're going to find out in a few minutes anyway from Rich. Why not get us ahead of the game? We won't tell anyone you said anything." He gave a gentle elbow into Irving's ribs. "Right?"

"Right." Irving rubbed his chest. "Or you could learn a little patience. It could do you some good."

"What are you trying to be? My father or something?" Skuz crossed his arms.

"He's trying to teach you a valuable life lesson, mate," Kelly said. "Trust me, you'll know soon enough. It won't be anything outside your skill set though. That I trust."

"Whatever. If you want to be stingy, fine." Skuz grumbled to himself until suddenly his eyes lit up. "Where's Walter? I bet he'd know what's happening."

"He'd tell you the same thing. He's more of a hardass than me."

Both of Skuz's hands went up to his head and he turned around and muttered incoherent curses.

Irving rolled his eyes. "Ignore him. He's a little too antsy for his own good."

Walter wandered out of the building behind the main house and raised his hand when he saw them.

"What are you cunts doing here today?" He wandered over and stopped a few yards away. He stuck his hands in his pockets and swayed back and forth. "Not that I'm complaining."

"We were called over by your boss," Irving said. He looked over at Skuz. "Some of us are better at waiting than others."

Walter looked over at Skuz pacing. "Is that the guy Garret always hangs out with? Interesting hair. I always heard stories, but I never imagined a purple mohawk could look that lame and feral."

"What did you say?" Skuz sprinted over and stopped.

"Now you've done it." Irving covered his eyes with a hand and shook his head. "He won't stop now."

"Damned right I won't. See, the purple hair is often misunderstood. Many people think -"

The main building's door opened. Richard and Eric emerged. Richard spoke up. "Spare them. I'm tired of hearing that crap."

"You're lucky," Irving laughed. "He'd have gone on for hours."

"So, what's up, Pres?" Skuz asked. "These jackasses won't tell us anything."

"We now know exactly who that shot caller is. You won't believe it."

"Don't leave us in suspense now," Skuz said. "Who is it?"

"That's ES-15's second in command. I'm talking second only to their supreme leader."

"Are you going to change the plan with Garret and the others? Now would be the time," Skuz said. "They're probably watching them right now. In a few hours they'll be executing the plan, and it'll be too late."

"Abandon it?" Richard threw his head back and let out a hearty laugh. "No, never. This is precisely the opportunity we've been looking for. If we take him out, the leader himself will have to either send even more resources and manpower or take the loss."

"You need any help from us, brother?" Eric asked. "If you're doing something, I can send someone to help you out. How about I send Mr. Kelly to accompany you. He knows how to get important things done."

"For what it's worth, Pres, I think his skill set would come in handy for this," Irving said.

"He's right," Kelly said. "I'm up for it."

"Sure. We could always use a master persuader," Richard said. "Just know it'll be a few hours before we acquire your subject."

"Why the wait?" Eric asked.

"Our team is studying his movements for the first opportunity to grab him. He exposes himself three times a day like clockwork. We don't want to rush it."

"Smart," Eric grinned. "Yeah, Kelly, you're going with them. Do whatever they say, within reason. Show them how we get answers."

Kelly showed a toothy smile. "Sure thing, boss. I've been looking forward for a chance to exercise my skill set lately anyway."

Outside the restaurant...

"Why can't we turn the air conditioning on?" Ann whined from the back. She fanned herself using her hand. "We've been here for hours. The last time we saw him was hours ago. No one will notice our engine running for a little cold air."

"It's exposure we don't need," Tony said. He tossed a

bottle of water back to her. "Drink that and don't dehydrate. You'll be fine. It's why we brought the cooler with us."

"Why do you all have to do things the hard way?" She took a big swig from the bottle. "At least we know he's on schedule today, since you saw him earlier."

A vibration in Garret's pants pocket caused him to withdraw his phone and look at the screen. "Oh my God."

"What is it, bro?" Tony asked, leaning over and trying to peek at the screen. "Oh shit, son. Is that for real?"

"Now you've got me curious." Ann leaned forward and looked over Garret's shoulder. "Holy balls around Saturn! Is he being serious?"

"Rich does not joke about things like this," Garret said. "The plan stands, but at least now I guess we know who we're kidnapping. It changes nothing."

"You're right." Tony brought up a hairy arm and looked at his watch. "He should be here soon. No sense in getting spooked by a little rank, right?"

"Damned right," Garret said. He brought the binoculars up to his eyes. "Hold up a minute. That might be him. It's a similar car. Yeah, he's getting out. It's definitely him." He tossed the tool down near his feet. He turned around in his seat and locked eyes with Ann. "Ready for some fresh air?"

"Now you're speaking my language." Ann finished off the water bottle and wiped her mouth. Her hand reached for the handle. "Same plan as before? I distract him, you grab him, and Tony approaches?"

"Yes."

"Let's go then before this opportunity passes us by. I'm not getting stuck in here for seven more bloody hours." She threw open the door and jumped out onto the pavement.

Garret stepped out of the car and, before slamming the door shut, spoke to Tony. "As soon as you see us talking to the guy, start your approach. We want out of here as soon as we're ready. No delays."

"I got your back."

Garret nodded and shut the door. He turned to Ann. "Don't deviate from the plan this time please."

"My improvisations always worked out before. Don't you remember when I helped you get your best friend back?" she asked walking beside him on the sparsely populated sidewalk. "You need to trust me more. It's essential for any long-term relationship. Didn't your mamma ever teach you how to treat women?"

"Let's just go with no." Garret looked over at the restaurant, away from Ann.

"Sore issue?"

"We can talk about this tonight after we're out of mortal danger right outside our biggest rival's cash cow."

"You're no fun sometimes," Ann pouted with her lips pursed. "You need to learn how to live a little. I was just trying to learn a little about my boyfriend. Is that so wrong?"

They circled around the front of the restaurant as they talked. "Ordinarily, no. These are special circumstances."

"Maybe I'm a special kind of girl." She reached over and pinched his hip.

"You'll get no argument from me on that." He grabbed her nearest hand and pulled her close.

"You know, one day you're not going to be able to escape these difficult conversations so easily," she squeezed his hand and slapped his behind, "honey buns."

They turned the corner and saw their target's car parked next to the single door at the back of the building. "I guess I'll wait here." Garret pulled out his phone and leaned back against the wall.

"You're just going to loiter?"

"I have a phone." He held it up to her. "No one's going to give me shit if they know what's good for them. I'm just another Joe Shmo who loves his phone too much." He kicked his foot up against the wall and focused his attention on the device.

"Typical lazy male behavior." Ann glared at him and saw that he never lifted his gaze, and only a small smile lingered on his face. "You suck."

"You sound bitter. I'd focus more on your job than how I whittle my time away. You focus on your job - I'll focus on mine." He rolled his eyes. "Women."

She glared at him and turned the corner. She passed the van and turned around. When she heard a door opening, she began again and saw the target coming toward her. She pretended to trip and fell to her knees. "Ah," she grunted and cradled her ankle. "What am I going to do now?" She tilted her head up and saw her target offering a hand down. She took it and stood up. She wobbled a bit and placed a hand on his shoulder.

"¿Estas bien? La caída te ha tenido que doler."

"Uh, habla ingles?" she asked.

He cleared his throat. "Sorry, miss." he replied in a suave latin voice. "My mother tongue just slips out. Are you okay though?" He looked down at her ankle. He kneeled and leaned in to examine her foot. "You didn't hurt yourself did you, little lady?"

Ann looked over the man and saw Garret watching the two. She smirked and looked down at their mark. "You are far too kind, sir."

"Nothing looks harmed." He stood up with a smile. "Shall I escort you to a doctor? I know a great one nearby that takes walk-ins if you have someone vouch for you. I'd be glad to do so."

She brought a hand up to her chest. "Really? For me? You are far too kind. I can take care of..." She took a step forward and stumbled into his grip. "I guess not."

She peeked over his shoulder and saw Garret visibly shaking and growling. She looped one arm around the man's shoulder and beckoned Garret over with her index finger. "I'm very sorry, sir. I don't mean to keep you." She looked down at her shoes."

"Do not worry about it, miss." He wrapped an arm around her shoulder and supported her weight."

"Hey, buddy, do you have the time?" Garret asked from behind him.

"Hm?" the shot caller asked with a turn of his head. He was met with a fist slamming into his cheek. He tumbled to the sidewalk as a van screeched to a halt beside them on the street. The back doors flung open along with Tony's voice. "Get him in here quick."

Garret grabbed his legs, only to receive a kick in the stomach for his trouble. "You bastard."

"Hijo de puta." He attempted another kick from the ground when a shadow overtook his view. He looked up to see Ann towering over him. He reached a hand up. "Please, miss, help me."

"Okay then," she said. She pulled out a small cloth and wrapped it over his nose and mouth. His eyes went wide until they closed, and he ceased moving. "Now let's get him in here before anyone sees." She helped Garret drag him into the back of the van, then climbed inside herself alongside Garret.

The van rolled off. Garret opened the toolbox in the corner of the cabin and retrieved a long length of chains. He flipped him over and tied his hands together behind his back. He tossed a length of chain to Ann. "Get his feet. I don't want another bicycle kick." He rubbed his solar plexus.

"Your plan was to what exactly?" she asked wrapping the chain around the man's feet. "Knock him out in one strike?"

"Not originally." Garret scurried back against the cabin's walls.

"What changed it then?" she asked.

"Probably when he saw you getting chummy with the dude is my guess," Tony said from up front. "It'd have pissed me off."

"Is that true?" Ann slid closer to Garret with a toothy grin. "Were you jealous over little old me? Did I fool you too?"

He elected to not answer her with audible words. He merely looked over at her.

"That's a yes."

8

Tony turned off the main road and steered down the twisty dirt path. "We're almost there. It's just another few minutes till we're good. You may want to wake him up now."

"Good idea," Ann said. She glared down at the unconscious man near her feet. She swung her right foot back and forwards, landing in the crook of his shoulder. The body rolled toward Garret with a thud.

Muffled words filled the cabin as he looked up at Garret and over at Ann.

"Don't get too excited now." Garret placed his foot on top of his chest and pushed down. "You're not going anywhere we don't want you to. We just didn't want you to miss all the fun. We've pulled out all the stops just for you. We even brought someone to entertain you. Aren't you excited?"

"We even invited some guests to this little pow-wow," Tony said from the front. "Word is the Outback Boys' best and brightest is waiting on us. He's here specifically to talk to you. You should be honored."

The man below shook his head and tried to roll away, only to be stopped by another pair of feet. Ann placed hers a lot lower than Garret had. "I'd stop moving if I were you, unless you don't care about a certain part of your anatomy. The boys here are too squeamish for such things." She leaned forward. "I'm not, sweetie."

He stopped attempting to roll and instead elected to look back between the three of them from his vantage point on his back.

"That's a good boy," Ann cooed. "See, boys? It just takes a woman's touch."

"We're here. I see the boys ahead." Tony pumped the brake and slowed the van as they approached an opening in the sparse forest. A line of bikes impeded their progress. A small car was plugging the side of the road with a license plate that read AUSSE. "We're as far as we can go. Time to walk." He brought the van to a stop and pulled out the keys. He twisted around in his seat and glared at their prisoner. "Your day's about to get a hell of a lot worse." He chuckled to himself. "Now let's get him out here already."

"You don't have to tell me twice." Garret stood up from his sitting position and threw open the back doors. He hopped out and turned around. He extended his hand toward Ann who took it. "Easy does it."

"If I didn't know any better, Mr. Price, I'd think you were almost a gentleman," Ann said.

"I'm always a gentleman." He looked back and reached inside. He wrapped his hands around the man's ankle and dragged him out. He looked to his side. "Dear, would you mind helping me with this luggage?"

"You'd be lost without me." She took the other foot and yanked. Once his legs had cleared the edge, she dropped his foot.

Tony tapped her shoulder. "I've got it from this point."

"I'll leave it to you two then." Ann wandered off toward the group past the other side of the barricade of bikes. "Just don't take too long. I don't want to wait for this entertainment too much longer."

"I hear that." Garret pulled the tied-up man into a standing position. "Hurry up, or we'll drag you."

The man got to his feet and shuffled forward under the guiding hands of Garret and Tony. They passed the motorcycle barricade and ambled toward the group. Ann fell in behind the two.

"It took you three long enough." Skuz waved to the group. "We thought the show was never going to start."

"There're the diggers now," Kelly said in his unmistakable Australian accent. "I can't believe you actually managed to catch the cunt."

The man stopped as soon as he saw Kelly. His eyes went wide. Beads of sweat rolled down his face, and he shook his head with a loud muffled grunt.

"Get over there." Garret pushed him forward down onto the dirt path. "Don't be so rude toward our guest." He waved Kelly over to them. "It seems this guy knows who you are, my friend."

"That doesn't surprise me." Kelly kneeled then looked up at Ann. "With all due respect, Sheila, I recommend you take a literal hike. You're not going to want to see this when we start."

"Don't call me Sheila. Besides, you underestimate me, sir."

"On your head be it. Don't blame me for your future nightmares." He grabbed one of the man's legs and dragged him. "Help me out."

Garret dropped the arm and jogged forward to grab the other leg. "I've been waiting to see these skills in action."

"You'd better take notes." Kelly dropped the leg once they got him in the middle of the entire gang. "Now what's first, lads?" He reached down and ripped the tape off his mouth. "You feel like talking?"

"Vete al demonio," he spat out.

"What was that?" Richard asked.

"I think he just told us to go to hell," Kelly smiled, replacing the tape. "We'll see how long that bravado lasts. It always fades eventually. The trick is applying the right amount of pressure." A muscled arm pulled out the knife at his side and raised it toward the sky. He rotated it as he talked. "Some men require more persuasion than others, but they all crack. It's just a matter of poking, prodding, and bending joints until they reach that point."

"Right then," Richard said. "Let's get started. We've got some chain. Let's tie him to that tree and get this show on the road." He pointed behind the group to a large sturdy tree.

"Got it." Garret and Kelly dragged him over to the tree with the chain sitting on the ground beside it. They stood his immobile form up and Kelly held him in place while Garret set about tying him to it.

"You're in for a treat, mate," Kelly said. "I haven't got to test my skills in over a year now. I've been waiting for just such an occasion."

"Let me have first crack at it before you go wild," Garret said with a last twist of the chain, securing their victim to the trunk of the tree. He circled around to the front. "You know how this is going to go. Let's not make this unpleasant for everyone involved. Answer my questions, or you get to experience a level of pain your little cartel buddies can only dream of inflicting." He ripped off the tape from his mouth.

He responded only with spitting on Garret's chest.

"That's how you're playing it, huh? I guess they never said you cartel types were intelligent in the least." He turned around to the group. "Go get the toolbox from the back of the van. I need them to loosen his tongue."

"I'll get it." Skuz ran off towards the van and disappeared inside the back. He reappeared and jogged over with the red box. He placed it down and opened it. "What are you thinking of using, buddy? The screwdriver? The pliers? Tell us what you're thinking."

Garret got to his knees and rummaged through the box until he pulled out a flat head screwdriver. "I'm going to get a little creative. No one will hear him out here, right?" He turned back and sauntered over. He grabbed one of the man's hands. "Last chance before it starts. Feel like talking?"

"No."

"Simple, but fine." Garret jammed the flat head underneath his victim's fingernails. "How about now? Maybe a little leverage would change your mind?"

"Te voy a matar."

"What did he say?" Garret looked back at the group.

"I think he said he was going to kill you," Ann said. She came up beside Garret. "That's not very nice. What happened to that guy who helped me up when I fell? He was helpful."

"Don't say I didn't warn you, asshole." Garret applied pressure as the man screamed at the top of his lungs. The nail from his index finger dangled, barely connected by the time he was done. "Now for the fun part. Still don't feel like talking?"

He didn't give an audible response, merely a shake of his head.

"You want the honors?" he asked Ann.

"Torture's not my bag. I prefer to watch." Ann sat down on the soil and leaned her neck back. "By all means provide me with some entertainment."

"That I can do." Garret reached and grabbed the hanging keratin with his free hand. "You don't need this anymore." He ripped off the hanging nail amidst another yell. "Don't be such a big baby. Fingernails aren't essential, they just hurt to lose. My next step will be far worse. Feel like sparing yourself that torment yet?"

"He's not budging, mate." Kelly cracked his knuckles. "Why not let me have a shot this round?"

"Fine. I'll tag out. Don't mutilate him too much. I want another shot."

Kelly took a step forward and dug through the toolbox. "No worries. I know how to play with others." He pulled out the pliers. "I just got a wicked idea," he said with a devilish grin. He stomped up to the tree. He wrapped the tool around an earlobe of the unfortunate man. "Still don't feel like talking, boy?"

"Puta madre."

"I'm going to assume that's a no. You don't really need those ears then, do you? They'd only be wasted on a guy who never hears anything worth telling." He clamped down on the cartilage and yanked hard.

Tony looked away. "That ain't right. Ears aren't supposed to do that."

"He deserves every second of this." Lucien never took his eyes off the display. "Remember what they did to Irving and Vinny."

Kelly grunted in exertion as he placed his foot against

the tree and pushed back hard until the stretching cartilage snapped and an ear-piercing scream broke the relative quiet. Kelly opened the pincers and let the flesh fall to the soil beneath to accompany the droplets of blood now dripping down from the shot caller's ear. "Just know this doesn't end until you do talk. You're going to get more and more mutilated until you tell us what we want to know. There is no way out. Your own group doesn't even know you're here. They're not going to roll up and rescue you. Does that put it in perspective now, you piece of shit?"

Garret stepped forward and placed a hand on Kelly's shoulder. "My turn. Now what should be next?"

"If I may make a suggestion?" Ann reached inside the toolbox. "I think this would be effective." In one motion she removed her hand from the box and handed over the hammer. "Take his shoes off."

"I see where you're going," Garret smirked. He got down and took off the man's boots. He tossed them to the side. He leaned back and took hold of the hammer. "We're going to break every bone in your feet unless you start talking right now. I would recommend not cussing us out in Spanish again if you know what's good for you." He rested the round end of the hammer against the front of the feet. "No? Fine then. Just don't blame me for you being a cripple the rest of your life. Let's hope the cartel has a good medical program, because you're going to need a few months recovery. I'm sure they won't just shoot you and leave you in a ditch somewhere, right?" He swung his arm back and stopped only when one word from his captive broke his silence.

"Wait."

Garret stopped his swing and looked up. "You better feel like sharing."

"What do you want to know?"

Richard stepped forward and stood beside Garret. "It's about time. Tell us where your boss is? Is he up here or south of the border?"

"I don't know that kind of intel."

"You're saying a shot caller doesn't even know where his bosses are? I call bullshit. Garret, show him what happens when he lies to us."

"You got it, Pres." He swung his arm forward causing the hammer to connect with the top of the foot. A loud cracking noise followed, along with a howl of pain. Garret stood up and took a step back. "You aren't going to be walking anytime soon with that."

"Alright, enough of this." Kelly took a step forward. "I have a method that's guaranteed to get him talking."

"Do share. What's that?" Richard asked.

"It's old school, but, in my experience, it works." He reached down to his belt line and extracted a large knife out of the holster. He stepped forward and rested the tip of the blade against his remaining ear. "First, I'm going to cut off your other ear, then your fingers, and then your toes. If you still don't feel like talking, I'll start moving to bigger parts that aren't essential. Maybe you only need one foot. Not that it'd do much good without any toes." He pushed the blade further into the cartilage. "Start talking or I start sawing off body parts."

"Alright man, I'll talk. You wanted to know where the big boss was, right? I only know today's plans. They make a new one every day."

Kelly pressed the knife deeper into the cartilage, now drawing blood. "You'd best get specific quick."

"Fine, he's in the city right now. Is that what you wanted to know?"

Richard stepped forward again, this time placing an arm

on top of Kelly's, halting him. "Where in the city is he, and how long is he staying?"

"Until there's a problem, old man."

"Which means if they know this conversation happened, he'll bolt," Garret said.

"Where is he?"

"If I tell you, they'll kill me."

Richard took his arm off Kelly's arm and patted his shoulder.

Kelly sawed off the cartilage until eventually he ripped it off with his hand. "Mate, you have far bigger problems to worry about right now. Unless you want to go home a featureless blob, you'll keep talking."

"My life's over anyway." Their prisoner's head drooped down. "If you don't kill me, they sure will for talking."

"Oh, don't say that," Richard said in his best jovial voice. "We're not the same as your group. We don't kill for the fun of it, only when necessary. We always fulfill our word. If you talk, we'll let you go after we finish our business with him."

"That wouldn't matter. I'd still be dead when they got a hold of me."

"What's your name?" Ann asked.

"What? Jose."

"Well, Jose, how about this? I'll smuggle you out of the country if you talk. They'll never find you if you cooperate. I'm not talking Mexico. I mean, how does a trip to Europe sound?"

Jose's eyes danced left and right. He bit his lip. "Can you actually make that happen?"

"How the hell did Sheila get him in a talking mood when we couldn't?"

"I guess you catch more flies with honey than vinegar," Garret shrugged.

"If you yank our chains though," Ann pounded a fist into an open palm, "I'll continue this questioning myself. Believe me, I'm not nearly as gentle as these two."

Garret and Kelly looked at each other. "Gentle?" they asked in unison.

"Tell us what we want first," Ann growled.

Jose sighed with a shaky breath. "Fine. The boss is holed up outside of the city limits to the north of town. He's there with about a half dozen bodyguards, so have fun with those guys."

"The boss left Mexico?" Lucien asked from the crowd. "The war in Mexico must be going worse than I thought. Running away like that's almost an admission of defeat."

"What's the name of the place they're staying at?" Ann asked. He looked back and pointed at the van. She snapped her fingers with only a single word. "Map."

Skuz jogged off to the van and returned with a map. He handed it to her.

"It's not a store. It's a simple white house with a chain fence. Do you think he'd be dumb enough to stay at a front?"

"Do you really want us to answer that?" Richard asked.

"I'll give you this one for free. Don't underestimate that old codger. He's wily and dangerous. He may be frail, but he's downright malicious."

"Warning noted," Kelly said. He jammed his knife beside Jose's head into the bark. He took the map from Ann and held it in front of her. "Now tell us which building it is, and you're done for the day."

Ann pointed at a house to the north of the city, only to be met with a shake of Jose's head.

"It's further out of town." His eyes followed her finger tracing the paper. "Stop. That one right there."

Ann looked at the map. "Is that so? That makes sense." She pressed the paper on the tree next to Jose, reached into her pocket and took out a pen. She circled the indicated house and walked over to Richard before handing over the map. "Here it is."

"Nice work." Richard slapped her shoulder and folded the paper up. He stuck it into his front pocket and looked up. "Now, what should we do with you?"

"I thought you were going to smuggle me into Europe?"

"No way, Jose," he said with a chuckle. "She promised that. You're right." Richard kept a hand on Ann's shoulder. "The problem is, she's not a club member."

"You motherfucker." Jose struggled against his binds.

"Rule number one is know your enemy, Jose," Garret said. "Too bad you went in blind and got taken for a fool." He turned around to the group. "Is the hole ready?"

"Damned right it is." Tony cradled his lower back. "We were here all morning digging."

"You're not going to…"

"Yes, we are," Richard smiled. His eyes trailed down Jose's body. "Too bad about that foot injury, or you might have had more of a chance of climbing out. Guess you should have talked earlier. Take him down and get him ready."

"It'll be our pleasure," Garret said. He and Kelly began the arduous task of undoing his bindings. "Get ready for him to drop."

No sooner had Garret said that then the chains went limp and Jose tumbled to the grass below.

"No time to rest." Ann reached down and grabbed him by the arm. She looked over her shoulder. "Skuzzy, help me with this trash."

"I guess it's only fair since I took the least shifts digging."

He stepped forward and grabbed the remaining arm. The two dragged him off toward the far end of the clearing. They stopped in front of a large open grave. "Guess where you'll be sleeping."

"Feel free to jump out before we finish loading the dirt back in though." Skuz stood up and laughed out loud.

"You can't do this," Jose said. He inhaled and exhaled quickly as he spoke. His head swiveled across the whole group. Sweat flung from his skin with every turn. "I'll tell you everything I know. Just don't do this."

Richard stepped toward him. He cradled his chin on his thumb and rubbed his cheek with his index finger. "See, the problem with that is now you're liable to lie. You're just not trustworthy anymore. You really should have talked earlier like we recommended." He extended his foot and rested the heel of his boot on Jose's chest. "Now take a nice long dirt nap." He looked to his right. "Put more tape on his loudmouth."

Tony strode up to the pair and ripped off a length of duct tape before adhering it to Jose's mouth. "With pleasure. I was getting tired of hearing this bitch beg, after being a pain in the ass."

Richard extended his foot and kicked Jose back into the dirt ditch. A puff of dirt floated up along with the sounds of muffled moans. "We got what we need. Now to just clean this up." He reached over to the side toward the multitude of shovels sticking out of the ground. "The sooner we start, the sooner we're done. Grab a shovel, you lazy bastards."

Everyone present, minus Lucien, grabbed a shovel and dumped piles of dirt into the open grave. Lucien stood at the head of the hole and peered over into it. "At least being old has some perks."

"Get us some water out of the cooler, old man," Richard

grunted. "Make yourself useful instead of laughing the whole time."

"I guess it'd be the least I can do." Lucien shrugged and went over to the van. He leaned into the back and dragged out the red cooler. He carried it over near the group and set it down. "There, first come, first served." He opened the box and took out a bottle.

Garret and Kelly approached the group with the chains in hand. "Hold up. I've got an idea."

"Make it quick." Richard wiped away sweat from his brow.

"No doubt." Garret jumped down into the grave and signaled to Kelly. "Come on."

"What's the plan, lad?" Kelly asked

"We can't risk him actually getting out of this."

"I got you. I'll take his arms then, and you get his legs." He punched Jose in the shoulder. "Stop moving so much." He looped the chains around Jose's upper body before tying it closed.

In the meantime, Garret tied both his feet together. "There we go. Now let's get out of this pit." He climbed out of the pit and turned around. He extended a hand down to Kelly and pulled him out. "Hand me that shovel, boss." He reached over to Richard. "I got this."

Richard handed the tool over with a small smile. "He won't be getting out of that without help."

"Not like he deserves any better." Lucien spat into the hole. His spit landed squarely on Jose's cheek.

"Hey, look." Skuz pointed down into the grave, "He's nearly covered."

"He's still kicking around. That means he can still breathe. We're a long way from done."

"We should have gotten a damned bulldozer," Tony groaned. "At least then we'd be done by now."

"And on a list. They make you sign those things out," Richard said. "It never was an option, as much as I wish it was."

With every shovel full of dirt, Jose's form became more obfuscated. His movements got slower. His grunts became quieter as he disappeared under the dirt.

"At least with all of us it's faster than just half of us." Skuz hefted another pile into the hole.

"Enough about that." Richard sat down on the bare ground beside the grave. "We need a plan for these guys."

"We could always go in with guns blazing for this guy," Skuz said. "If he's the big kahuna, who's going to order the retaliation? His third in command who'll be swamped, given their current situation south of the border? Word is they're losing turf at an astonishing rate down there."

"That actually may not be a terrible idea, given where he's holed up," Richard said. "Still, it's too bloody for my taste. He still has a few bodyguards. A stray bullet would hurt us just as much with our numbers. We need a smarter play here."

"There's only so many ways we can get a guy out of a building if he doesn't want to leave," Lucien said. "You either go in there after him, or you wait until he leaves."

"There is a third option," Ann said from outside the circle of men. "Just saying, I have an idea."

"Spit it out," Richard said.

"Have someone watching him for a night, and at the same time launch a fake attack. You'll be able to judge how many he has at his command. If he sends out anyone from his own place, you'll know they're in really dire straits. If not, then that's still more info. Then we could alter the plan to be more drastic."

"I like the sound of drastic," Skuz said. "What exactly does that mean?"

"It means not everything needs to be settled with guns and bullets. There are ways of eliminating threats without all the noise, and it will look natural; meaning, very little investigation."

"It's a huge risk sending people to watch their boss though," Kelly said. "If they did find out they were there, they'd shoot first."

"Then you'd better send your best liar and someone who would blend in."

"Wait a minute." Garret stopped digging. "You don't mean you?"

"I did save your ass repeatedly. What's exactly is wrong with me going?" Her hands fell to her hips and she huffed.

We'll talk about that later when we're alone. For now, sure. I have no problem with it."

"It's settled then," Richard said. "Garret and his girl-friend will sit a good distance away from that building and watch them. We'll give them something to panic about and see what they do."

Lucien wandered over from the rapidly filling hole. "I'll give Irving a call and update him."

"While you're at it, get him to dig up as much as he can from this place we're going," Garret said. "That is, if he's not too busy whipping the prospects into shape."

"I'll let him know. You two," he placed hands on both Ann and Garret's shoulder, "be careful, and stop bickering so much. You're going into the belly of the beast."

Ann snuck a glance at Garret and looked down at Lucien's shoes. "Fine."

Garret looked away and muttered something too low to be heard.

"You'll have to repeat that. I don't have a hearing aid."

"I said I just don't want her hurt, old man."

A wide smile emerged onto Lucien's face along with a laugh. He looked back to Ann. "No helping that."

"Now let's get going already." Ann grabbed Garret's hand and dragged him away from the group. "One of you can catch a ride with someone else, right?"

"Not it." Skuz said.

"What?" Tony asked after dumping another shovel full of dirt.

"I'm not riding bitch."

"You will if I tell you to. They were my ride."

"They said they'll be fine," Kelly called out. "This dill said he'd catch a ride with me." He pointed at Skuz at his side. "I just hope those two manage to pull it off." He watched them run off.

"Catch you later." Garret climbed into the driver's seat and waited for Ann to get seated beside him.

She poked her head out the window. "Have fun, boys."

Later on the side of the road...

"Can you see anything?" Ann asked. "It's just a normal looking two-story house. How are we supposed to get any kind of information like this?" Her hand bounced off the arm rest at her side.

"I have an idea, but it requires their phone number."

"I guess you should have asked for this place's number."

"There are other ways to figure that out you know." His

eyebrows jumped up and down. "Depending on how gutsy you are."

"Speaking of which, why didn't you want me here? I didn't hear what you said before."

"It's the same reason it's always been. I don't like you being on the front lines here. I know you're more than capable, but it turns out most people don't want their significant other to be in danger. I'm not different."

"Do you think I'm any different in that regard?" she asked. "You think I like watching you do all these jobs with only Skuz to help?" She reached over and tweaked his nose. She leaned over toward him. "No. So I understand it. Just know I do what I want. You'll get used to it eventually, or you won't. Either way, it's not changing."

"I'm still getting used to it. Most of my exes were the dainty type. You know what I mean?"

"Like the persona Katie put on? Yeah, I'm a different animal though, as you're aware."

"I'll get used to it eventually. Just don't get too angry at my concern." He reached over and engulfed her smaller hand in his own. "It's not exactly in my nature to begin with."

A brilliant blush stained her cheeks, and she looked away. "How can we get that number?"

"I'm glad you asked." He patted his chest. "I'm wearing my patch, so I can't do this."

"You're saying it involves me?"

"That's right. It goes against everything in my body, but I know I can't pull it off. It involves you sweet talking them or their neighbors. Do you think you can do that twice in a day?"

"I doubt their neighbors would know. They're keeping a low profile if they have two brain cells to rub together," she said. "Which means your little plan won't work. They're not going to tell us their number."

"You don't think a young, sexy, flirting woman would loosen their mouths?"

"Maybe if their boss wasn't in the same building. We can't help that though." She snapped her fingers. "I got it. We used to have a little trick that not many people knew about, though they should." She leaned over and reached a hand into Garret's pants pocket.

"Hey."

"Be quiet. You know you like it." She pulled out his phone. "You know what that is?"

"Enlighten me."

"You can find out anything on the internet. All we do is call Irving, hope he's not still doing whatever for Richard, and get him to look it up. He may have to pay like five to ten dollars, but it's worth it."

"Good idea. Maybe he can tell us who the previous owners were while he's at it."

"What good would that do?" Ann asked, dialing.

"Because maybe they didn't just buy it off Joe Schmo. It's hard to say what importance it'd have if we don't know who owned it in the first place."

"Fine, I'll ask. Yeah, could you put Irving on the phone, Harold? No, I can't wait." Her left eye twitched. "I tried to be nice, but for fuck's sake just put him on the phone. This is important."

"Give it here for a sec." Garret extended an open palm. She placed the phone in his grasp.

"Do what she says, or I will personally make your life a living hellscape of torment you will never escape. You think following Irving is tiring? You'll see what he underwent when I was training prospects. Does that sound fun? Do it."

He said with steel lining his voice. He passed the phone back. "There you go."

"Irving?"

"What's up? The prospect said it was important."

"He'd better have. We need your expertise for a moment. Are you near the computer?"

"It's where I spend most of my time until this damned cast is off," Irving said. "What do you need - prices, info, or something in particular?"

"We need a phone number. I'll text you the location. Can you do that for me please?"

"Of course. It shouldn't take more than a few minutes, assuming they have a landline. I'll give you a text with it. Be right back." The line went dead, and Ann looked over at Garret. "At least there's one good thing from him getting winged." She sent the address and leaned back in her seat.

"Who are we even going to get to call them anyway?" Garret asked. "I don't know Spanish. I doubt they have female agents."

"I know bits and pieces, but not enough to carry on a complicated conversation. Maybe we'll get lucky and they'll speak English."

"Fat chance. The lower rank and file may speak English, but as we've seen, the big timers are mostly speaking their native tongue."

"I guess you'll have to repeat after me and trust me. Can you do that?" Ann asked. A buzzing sound from Garret's pocket interrupted them.

He looked at the screen. "I have the number. He also said we could find this stuff out on our phone if we really wanted to not be lazy."

"We could," Ann said, "but it's not a good idea. There's a reason I called him and didn't open the web browser."

"Why is that?"

"Because our location is logged on public servers here. This thing still has gps I'm assuming, and everyone and their mother would know what we're looking up. It wouldn't be good if this ever went to court. At least this way we can get the info and still remain pseudo anonymous."

"That was Greek to me, but as long as it makes sense to you."

"Let's just say I did more than just physical security. Speaking of which, you should too. Sometimes the key to defense doesn't lie in the physical realm, it's waged in cyber-space. I'll have to teach you and Irving a little."

"Anyway, what should I say to whoever answers this?"

"We should have kept that dude alive and forced him to call. Don't you hate it when you forget minor details that would make things much easier?"

"Welcome to my life," Garret said in a flat voice. "I have an idea. How do you say, 'We're under attack at the restaurant and need reinforcements'?"

"Uh," Ann grabbed Garret's phone. "I think it goes something like 'Estamos bajo ataque en el restaurante. Necesitamos refuerzos'."

"How do you know that?"

"I just looked it up online. It's crude and probably a shit translation, but it's all we've got since we buried that guy."

"Fantastic." He took the phone back and dialed. He inhaled a deep breath as the third ring echoed in his ear.

"Hablar."

"Estamos bajo ataque en el restaurante. Necesitamos refuerzos." He immediately hung up. "Think they bought it?"

"Don't know. We'll see." She leaned forward and squinted her eyes. "Oh boy, hide." She reached over and looped her arm around Garret's neck. She pulled his face down to her lap. "It looks like they're sending a couple of guys out. Their car's coming near, act natural." She leaned her head back and kept a vice like grip on the back of Garret's head. She closed her eyes and let out a moan. She peeked out of the corner of her eye and saw the cartel's van sitting at a nearby red light a few feet away. One of their passengers was staring at their display out the window.

She winked at him and threw her head back again with a lascivious grunt.

The van moved forward as the light turned green. Ann let Garret up once they were clear.

"That was certainly interesting," Garret said, pulling away. "What the hell was that for?"

"You needed to be out of sight, and they were coming this way. Is it really complicated? If they saw that patch, we'd be fucked. All they saw was your hair."

"I guess that's true."

"Besides, a girl has to give hints some way."

"I'll make sure to remember that for tonight. Now that they're gone, I'll call Rich and tell him exactly how they scattered. We'll see what he has to say." He dialed another number and kept his eye on the building. "We're here, and they scattered after we called in an attack. What should we do?"

"How many are left in there?"

"No clue. They sent out two or three. Shall we try and end this war right now?"

"It's too dangerous. There could still be ten of them in there."

"We'll never know how many are in there. We may as well go now. If we're going to go, now'd be the time before they get back. We have like fifteen minutes to work with here."

"Dammit. Alright, fine. We're on our way. We'll take our bikes to bypass what traffic we can. You two, do what you feel is best. In case shit goes sideways, we'll come over. We'll park a few blocks away on our bikes and be ready for anything. Garret, be careful in there. If anything doesn't even smell right, I want you two out of there quicker than a lightning strike. Do you understand me?"

"I appreciate the concern, boss. I got it. We'll see you soon."

"What's the order?"

"Do what we feel is best. Care to end this war with me?"

"I've been wanting to kill that old man who enslaved Katie, and now is our best chance..." she trailed off. "Fine, count me in. How are we doing this?"

"We're winging it. We don't have time for a full plan right now, so let's get going. We'll figure it out as we go."

"That's a shit plan if I've ever heard one."

"Do you want revenge or not?"

"Of course I do." Ann pulled out her gun and checked her magazine. "I'm locked and loaded."

"Then let's head out. How are we getting inside?"

"You're asking me? I see a fence that leads up to a window if you climb it. I'd rather go in there than the front door. There's only one problem with that route."

"We're on the second floor with no real escape route in a pinch. No helping it though. It's the only way in. I guess we can always jump down to the grass below. It'll hurt, but it's the quickest way out."

"This has to be our dumbest play yet in the short time I've known you," Ann grumbled to herself.

"It's not ideal, but nothing ever is. If you don't want to go I'll go in alone, and you can keep the engine running."

"And leave me bored back here? Mr. Price, you have no tact with ladies. Fine. I'll go, to keep you alive if nothing else. Ready to go?"

"As ever." They both pushed open the doors and stepped outside. They fell in lock step beside each other down the sidewalk. They wrapped their arms around each other and ducked behind a nearby billboard out of sight of the building. "Now to just get close without drawing attention." Garret placed himself against the brick wall and looked ahead at the building. "Hard to do out here in the country."

"My middle name's subtlety," Ann smirked. "I have an idea."

"Lay it on me."

"Ever heard of 'fake it till you make it'? It also applies here. If we go up to that building looking all shifty eyed, we'll stick out like a sore thumb."

"I think that kind of fails when we climb up a fence, but the logic is sound for every other part."

"It's just to get near the building, not once we're inside of it, numb nuts." She gave a light punch to his shoulder. "So, act natural on our walk over. Just be a normal flirty couple, and even if they have lookouts, they won't notice much."

"They'll notice when they see we're getting too close. We'll just deal with them if it comes to it. We need to go now, so are you ready? They should be noticing that the call was false about now."

"Shit. I hate rush jobs," Ann said. "Fine." She curled up to Garret's side. "Let's go."

The pair swung around the corner and approached. The two laughed and clung to each other. They passed one jogger on the barren sidewalk. They finally crossed the last street and ducked into the nearby space between houses.

"Hurry over here." Ann scurried off toward the chain link fence.

"Ladies first."

"What a gentleman. You let me go first in a situation like this, but first thing in the morning you're always the first to the bathroom."

"You sure like to bring up the dumbest things when we're breaking and entering. Stay focused." He gave a light flick to her forehead. "Distractions get you killed."

She rubbed her forehead and opened her eyes to see Garret going up first. "So much for ladies first."

"I changed my mind. I figured I'd make sure it's safer for you." He looked down from climbing to wink at her.

"Now he decides to be chivalrous," she whispered to herself. She climbed up and teetered on the narrow metal line. "What are we waiting for?" she whispered.

"A dude's in there. I'd rather not shoot and announce our presence to the world if we can help it. It looked like he was watching a soccer match or something."

She climbed up and steadied herself. She peeked her head above and saw a man with his back to the window, staring at the screen on the other side of the room. "Let's hope it's not a squeaky window then. Keep your pistol trained on him. I'm going in. We're running out of time."

"Wait." He gripped her arm after she'd lifted the window a few inches. It screeched with every millimeter it raised. The two jumped down. They got low to the ground when they saw the man inside getting up from his seat and pressed themselves to the wall on either side of the window.

They could hear a voice from inside. "How'd he miss that shot?" The smell of nicotine reached their nostrils as puffs of smoke came from inside through the crack. "Everything's going to shit up here." Another wisp of smoke rolled out from the crack along with a buzzing sound. The man sighed, and a faint click echoed before he spoke again. "What? They have this location? Thanks for the heads up. I'll beef up security." Another click signaled he'd closed his phone. "Those idiot bikers think they're getting in here? They've got another think coming." An expended cigarette shot through the gap and fell through the grating to the grass below before the window was shut.

The pair waited a few seconds before daring to utter another breath. "How the fuck did he know we were coming?" Ann asked.

"Oh Christ."

"You know how?"

"We've got a rat somewhere."

"Which means we can't do anything until we find out who's informing them," Ann said. "I guess we're going rat hunting." She pointed down. "Now let's get back and start figuring this mess out. I don't want to be here any longer than I have to."

"Agreed." The pair slipped out of the property and headed back to their van on the main road. Once they reached the vehicle they pulled out into traffic.

"Who would it be? One of the prospects?" Ann asked.

"They wouldn't have enough intel to hurt us. We need to find out who else knew we were here and start our search there."

"I know you don't want to hear this, but it could be someone in the club."

"You're right," Garret said, his voice dejected. "I don't want to hear it."

"You can't discount the idea because it's unpalatable."

"I'm not," Garret snapped. "I just won't suspect them until I have good reason. If it's between them or one of the prospects, I say we investigate the prospects. You can follow which lead you want, but that's where I'm starting."

Garret pulled his phone out and speed dialed Richard's phone. "Yo, we're out in one piece."

"I was worried there for a second. We'll head back to the clubhouse and figure out our next move. Hold on a second. I'm getting a call from the clubhouse."

Garret heard a click and then silence. He glanced over at Ann driving. "I got put on hold."

Another click and Richard was back. "Get back to the clubhouse in a hurry. Something's happened. Irving said they were raided while we were away. Kelly was visiting, but Irving fended them off. The prospects ran when lead started flying."

"The cowards left an injured man to fend for himself? I'll beat some fucking sense into them when I get my hands on them." He gritted his teeth, and his voice was tense.

"You'll be waiting behind me, brother. I'll get my hits in first for that shit. They'll learn you never abandon a brother by the time I'm done with them."

"Executive privilege is a beautiful thing. We'll be right there."

"You want to tell me what happened?" Ann looked over. "Why are you so angry?"

Garret stuffed the phone into his pants pocket. "The clubhouse was hit while we were out. After the boys came to our defense, armed ES-15 busted in."

"Who left Irving?"

"Who do you think? The only ones still back there, the prospects."

"This does reinforce my theory though." She saw the

glare leveled at her out of the corner of her eye. "Don't look at me like that. It's true. Theoretically, the betrayer wouldn't want to be around when lead was flying."

"The prospects left him alone too, so I say it bolsters my idea."

"We'll see, won't we? I'll follow my leads, and you'll follow yours. We'll find out who was responsible for this mess. Trust me on that."

"You're damned right."

G arret busted through the door, his neck twisting back and forth with his .357 at the ready. "Irv? Buddy? Are you okay? It's us, Garret and Ann. Don't be shooting us now."

"Garret?" A lone hand reached up from behind the bar. It wobbled a bit as Irving's form ascended above the bar. "Thank Christ. I thought you were another one of those animals."

Garret ran over. "Jesus, dude." He threw Irving's arm over his shoulder and helped him over to one of the few unturned seats. "You're not supposed to be standing on your own yet."

"I didn't have much choice. It was scramble or have more lead introduced into my body. I chose the former." He sat down in the seat. "How the hell did they know when to hit us?"

"I wonder about that." Ann walked inside and closed the door behind her. "Did anyone act odd before they left?"

"Odd?" Irving asked. "That's awfully vague, but no, not really."

"No one was acting nervous?" She walked from one overturned table to the next and examined the wreckage.

"The only nervous ones I saw were the prospects. All but one of them freaked the hell out when shit started popping off. Harold was the only one with the sack to stay back with me."

"Where the hell's he at?" Garret asked. "I see he left."

"Because I ordered his fat ass to," Irving chuckled. "I wasn't going to get him shot trying to get my ass out."

"I'll have to exclude him from the beatings then." Garret clicked his tongue. "Still, how many were there?"

"As soon as they kicked the door in, they didn't wait. They started shooting." He pointed up at the mangled lights above. "As you can tell, it was more of a scare tactic, but damned if it didn't work on most of us. I told Ronald to get out the back and Cory was in the back already. I assumed he ran out that way. I was wondering if they got out alright? Did you see them on your way in?"

"No, bro, we didn't. If they were smart, they had men posted out back. Maybe they got away, maybe they didn't." He patted Irving's back. "We're just glad you're still okay. For a minute there, I thought we'd lost you again."

"I was lucky to get behind the bar before I caught a bullet. Harold was a big help with his distraction. He squeezed off a few rounds in their direction while I crawled to cover. Before I knew it, he slid into cover beside me."

"I'll have to buy him a beer," Garret said.

"We need to find Cory and Ronald." Ann crossed her arms with a frown. "Something smells fishy here."

"You don't think they had something to do with this?"

"You sweet summer child," Ann said. "Who else could have told them you'd be here alone?"

"They could have done the same thing we do - watch us

at all hours of the day. I mean we set a camera to watch their place all day and night. With their resources, they could have just made a guy post up nearby with a camera and lots of hard drive space on a laptop."

"Maybe," Ann said, "but my money's elsewhere."

"Ignore her. I'm with you. Either they've been keeping tabs, or Cory or Ronald tipped them off."

"Are you serious? They may be lazy, but that's no reason to suspect they're ratting us out."

"I wish it wasn't so, buddy, but someone or something told them this was the best time to strike."

"The cops will be here soon." Ann walked over to the door and peeked out the window. "There's no way someone hasn't called this in to nine-one-one yet."

"Just what we need. Another round of cops asking us asinine questions while we fall behind." Garret spat on the tiled ground. "It can't be avoided though. It'd just make us look worse. Just remember the golden rule with the cops, Irv."

"Never say anything and demand a lawyer."

"Good man."

"Here they come." A siren grew closer as red and blue lights swirled outside the building.

That night...

I thought they'd never leave." Garret watched the caravan of police cruisers leave single file out of their parking lot."

"Where're the guys at?" Irving asked. "Shouldn't they be back by now?"

"They probably saw the cops and stayed away, if I know

them," Garret said. "If they're still watching, they'll be back soon." His pocket vibrated. "Speak of the devil." He pulled out the phone and texted back. "They're on their way."

Garret walked back to the table Irving occupied and sat across from him. "It's got to be either Cory or Ronald."

"You really think they'd rat on us?"

"There's a reason they're prospects, not full members. Never fully trust a prospect if they haven't earned it, Irv. That's rule number one."

"Or he's mistaken." Ann pressed her face to the window facing the parking lot. "It's either that, or a member. No one else had the intel to hurt us to my knowledge."

The back door opened, and a haggard looking Ronald trudged back inside.

Garret's eyes darted over and he vaulted out of his seat. He sprinted over and grabbed a handful of his collar. "You want to tell me where you've been?" he asked through gritted teeth.

"What are you talking about?" His larger hand tried to pry Garret's hand away from his neck but failed.

"You left a brother in the middle of a shootout, and then have the gall to ask me why I'm pissed? You're either intentionally dense or stupid. Fine. What were you doing when it all went down? Answer me that."

"I was cleaning in the back," he gasped out.

"That's it?" Garret looked over to Irving. "Is he telling the truth?"

Irving slapped the side of his head. "Yeah. Also, now that I think about it, Kelly was here earlier. I sent Cory with him in the back in case he needed anything."

"Seriously? You just now remembered?"

"Sorry, man. It's been a busy day. Some things slip your mind. Cory was in the back with Kelly."

"When shit popped off, Kelly told me to follow him as he ran out the door, so I did."

Garret let him breathe a bit and loosened the pressure on his grip. "What about Cory? Where was he?"

"Hell if I know. He's always slacking off. The last I heard he was supposed to be taking out the trash to the dumpster out back. He probably bolted when he heard the shots, if I had to guess. Can you let me down, sir? It's getting hard to breathe."

Garret completely released Ronald and sighed. "Did Kelly make it out alright?"

"Yeah. I watched him get out myself. I was about to turn back inside when he dragged me off. He told me I'd just get myself killed if I went back in."

"He was probably right," Ann said, walking closer. "Do you even have a gun?"

"Yes, ma'am." His eyes fell to his belt line at his side.

She reached for it, ejected the magazine, and peeked. "It's loaded alright."

"Rich will deal with you when he gets back. For now, do you have any idea where Cory might be?"

"Probably at home? I don't know, sir. I don't ask about his personal life."

"Which means I have one more stop tonight before I head home."

"Count me in," Ann said. "I have a few questions myself."

The roar of motorcycles met their ears.

"You stay here, and don't run if you know what's good for you." Garret poked Ronald in his chest. He went back toward the tables while Ann stood staring at him from head to toe.

"If you did, it'd look awfully guilty." She squinted her eyes at him. "I'll be watching you."

The roar of engines stopped.

"I really don't think he had anything to do with it," Irving said.

The door opened and everyone filed in. Richard led the group. "Who? Jesus, my walls." Rich looked at the bullet damage. "Is everyone whole?"

"Irving's fine. The big man isn't hurt I see," Garret looked up and down Harold trailing in the back of Richard's entourage, "but we still have one MIA. Cory's gone and hasn't shown up yet. We think he ran when this all popped off. Ronald's story is Cory was taking out the trash when it went down."

"I'm guessing this was our favorite group?" Rich sat down with Irving.

"Bingo," Irving said. "I specifically heard Spanish being yelled at us before the gunshots."

"I'm glad you're alright," Richard said. "Now we have the cops watching us though. It's going to complicate matters from here on out."

"I want to go to Cory's house tonight and find out just where he was when this went down. Something doesn't smell right here," Garret said. "Either they're watching us, or someone told them when to strike."

"At this point, I wouldn't discount that they've set up surveillance too. Still, we need to cover all our bases." Richard looked over at Garret. "Go ahead and pay him a visit. Find out what went down. Don't go medieval on him until you have proof he ratted. Apply a little pressure, but nothing too bad." He glanced at Harold who was coming through the door. "How about the big man? What'd he do when this all happened?"

"He covered me until I ordered his fat ass to get out," Irving said. "Ain't that right, kid?"

"Yes, sir."

Richard nodded. "That a boy. You go with Garret, Harold. I bet you want those answers as much as he does, considering you almost died because of this."

"Yes, sir."

"Good, then it's settled. Garret's merry little band will cover that angle. While they're doing that, I'll give our allies a ring and see if they've heard anything. So far, they're one step ahead of us. We need to utilize all our resources if we want to stay ahead of the game."

"Take off your vest, prospect. You're with us." Garret took off his kutte and draped it over a nearby chair.

Harold followed orders and removed the vest. "Why?"

"So you don't give wandering cops or do gooders reason to call the police on us specifically," Lucien said. "Never commit crimes with your colors on. That's basic shit."

"Right."

"Do everything Garret and Ann say. They know how interrogation works," Richard said. "Make sure to bring all you'll need."

"Prospect, go load up one of the vans with a toolbox, some duct tape, and a pair of brass knuckles," Tony said. "Garret will need those for his little convincing session, if I know him."

"We have those?" Harold asked.

"Look in the storeroom, you idiot. The knuckles should be near the top shelf."

"Got it." Harold hurried as fast as his stocky form let him and disappeared into the stock room.

"Shall I call Kelly this time?" Richard asked. "He was a big help last time."

"Let's not call in all our favors in a hurry," Garret said. "The prospect bought us some more good will by sneaking him out the back earlier. Let's foster that a bit. We might need more firepower later, and we don't want them feeling like we owe them after all this. Right?"

"Good thinking. I'm pretty sure you can handle a prospect anyway."

"Damned right."

"Can I go?" Skuz asked. "You can't just leave me out of this, brother."

"We could use someone to watch the prospect in the car," Garret said. "We don't want him panicking and leaving us alone over there if something happens."

"Good thinking in covering your bases. Go with him, Skuz." He nodded in Garret's direction. "Make sure the prospect learns the basics while they're dealing with Cory. I mean everything. If you can think about it, lecture him about it. He's our most promising candidate thus far. We need him to know everything."

"I'll teach him everything I know."

"Hopefully you won't teach him your sense of fashion," Tony snickered. Soon the whole table was laughing out loud until Skuz spoke over them.

"I know you're just jealous of this." He rubbed his purple mohawk and the shaved sides of his head. "Ya'll need to stop lying to yourselves."

"We all have our transgressions," Garret said, sticking another cigarette between his lips. "Lying, in this case, isn't one of them."

"Got them." Harold huffed and puffed as he hurried back.

"We need to put you on a diet, if you're tired from just that." Garret flicked his lighter wheel down and the flame engulfed the end of his cigarette. "From now on, you're on a two thousand calorie diet, fat boy."

"Seriously?"

"Seriously," the entire group said in sync.

"Best get your calculator ready, because I'll be counting what you eat. If you're over, you'll get to run," Lucien said.

"For now, come on." Garret stood up. "Unless there's something else, we need to get going. I want to sleep sometime tonight."

"Just make sure to do it right. No alarms, no cops, and don't let him make too much noise."

"What do we do if he has an alarm system?" Harold asked. He looked left and right at the whole table. "What? I don't know how to disarm it. I'm not an electrician, and I doubt any of you are. Do we just abandon it if he has one?"

"Mm." Richard rubbed his chin with his hand. "You can always cut the power to the house."

"It's a moot point anyway," Irving said. "I've been there. He doesn't have a system. Good thinking ahead though. That'll serve you well eventually."

"It's settled. Get going."

"You heard the pres." Garret stood up along with Ann and Skuz. The three moved to the door. Garret opened it and let Ann go first. He looked back at the inside of the clubhouse. "Come on, prospect. It's time to pop your first operation cherry."

"I have a bad feeling about this," Harold muttered to himself before jogging to catch up to the three outside. The tools inside the red box clattered with every step. He eventually caught up with the trio and circled around the back of the nearest van in the parking lot. He pulled open the doors and slid the red box into the back. He climbed in beside them and closed the doors. He got on his knees and peeked over the seat. Reaching into his pockets, he passed ahead the brass knuckles to Ann.

"For me? You really know what a girl likes," she giggled. "Just kidding." She passed the weapon over to Garret. "Here."

"Do you know why we're visiting Cory, Harry?" Garret asked with a turn of the key.

"Uh, not really."

"When you tried to get Irv out earlier, did you realize where the other two were? I'm referring to Cory and Ronald," Skuz asked from just in front of Harold.

"Ronald was ordered away like me, from what I could decipher from all the screaming - not by Irving, but by Kelly. I don't know what happened to Cory."

"He ran like a bitch." Garret rested his arm out the window to his left and ashed his cigarette. "He left you and Irv by yourself, with no concern for your wellbeing."

"You don't do that," Skuz said. "When you join us, you take an oath. We protect each other through thick and thin. You already knew that subconsciously. That's why we're bringing you along. To see what happens when you abandon your brothers."

"He was probably just scared out of his wits. Is this seriously the way to deal with that?"

"He'll accept it, or he'll quit. Either he'll learn and overcome it, or he'll puss out," Skuz said. "Either way, the situation needs dealt with. We can't have a guy on the roster who would leave us out to dry because he pisses his pants every time something goes down. Do you get it now?"

"A little."

"Good."

The van started moving as Skuz kept talking. "You'll be with me in the van while those two work their magic inside." He kicked the seat in front of him. "Or do you two want him in there for a little extra muscle?"

"Stay here," Garret ordered Harold. "We wouldn't want to take away Skuz's chance to teach you everything you need to know, would we?" He took another drag from his cigarette. "Skuz, you'll be taking the wheel when we go inside."

"Got it."

"Don't get too caught up lecturing. I want you to be ready to get us out of there at a moment's notice."

"You know me - always paying attention."

Garret looked up into the rear-view mirror. "You'd better be." He reached down toward the radio knobs and twisted until a voice became clear.

"As you all know, recently a local man was murdered by a gunshot. Police at first didn't release any details, but our inside sources say it was a local man that immigrated here over a decade ago. Police aren't sure yet just why the man was targeted, but they're still investigating."

"They're talking about Yeltzin?" Skuz asked. "Do you think they'll put it together?"

"How could they?" Garret blew smoke out of the window to his left. "All they know is his head got blown up. They have no witnesses, no suspects, and not even a murder weapon. We got out clean, remember?"

"At least that's one problem solved," Ann said. "Now we have them breathing down the club's back with that little attack earlier." She angled herself to look behind. "Speaking of which, we have an admirer following us."

Garret checked the mirror on his left. "Think it's the cops?"

"That's my bet," Ann said. "They have no real proof on us, so they're probably watching us."

"Fuck." Garret bit his lips. "That changes things. We can't just lose them like we would any normal tail."

"Why not?" Harold asked.

"Because, retard, if we run a red light or pull a u-turn that'd just give them more ammunition," Skuz said. "There's only one way of dealing with this."

"We'll have to be on our best behavior when we get there."

"Or quiet," Ann said. "He probably had blinds on his windows, right?"

"We don't know he did this yet." Garret tossed the stub of a cigarette out the window into the grimy, water filled gutter. "We may have our suspicions, but we're there to find out - not pass judgement immediately."

"True that," Skuz said.

"Why not drop you both off then drive off?" Harold asked. "The cop would follow us I bet. If not, we could message you."

"That's actually a pretty good idea," Ann said. "It'd give us a little privacy."

"We'll lead him on a merry chase," Skuz said. "Hey, prospect, how do you feel about a little shopping trip?"

"Sounds good to me."

"It's settled then," Garret said. "We'll get out a few blocks up from his house, so he doesn't get suspicious."

"What will we do if he doesn't follow us?" Harold asked.

"Then we'll explain how we're just visiting a friend," Ann said. "Which we are, at least as far as he could prove."

"We'll say we were worried about him after today or some shit. Cops'll eat that up," Garret said. "We're almost there. Everyone ready?"

"Sure." Skuz unbuckled his safety belt as the van slowed down on the side of the road.

"He's slowing down too." Harold peeked over his shoulder.

"Then let's see which bait he takes." Garret threw his door open and stepped outside. Skuz took his seat without delay as Ann jumped out the back onto the sidewalk.

"Later, you two. Don't do anything I wouldn't do," Skuz said with a wave out the window.

Garret brought his attention to the cop car and watched it follow behind the van. "They took the bait. Let's head inside." Without waiting, he started walking the two blocks and approached the two-story house.

"Remember, we're not here to accuse him," Ann said, "just to see what happened."

"Right." Garret reached a hand up and banged on the door with all his might. He looked to his side only to hear the door open and a click from in front of him.

Garret swiveled his head back in time to see Ann's hand shoot forward, smacking the hand to the side. The semi-automatic handgun clattered against the brick and eventually down to the concrete at his feet. He reached down and grabbed the gun, while Ann wrestled her way inside and pinned him against the wall.

"Is there a reason you want me dead, prospect?" Garret stepped inside the foyer and closed the door behind him. "Spooked about something?"

"I was the one telling him to take it easy," Ann growled through her teeth. "That was until you leveled a gun at us."

"Stop!" An unfamiliar female voice said, along with a myriad of light steps coming down the nearby steps. "Let go of my brother." Her small form crashed into Ann and fell backwards onto her butt.

Garret grunted and looked over at the wannabe attacker

sprawled on the floor. "You're his sister I'm assuming." He took a step toward the small girl.

She scampered backward until her back hit the wall. "He may be an idiot, but please don't hurt him," she sniffed.

Garret looked back at Cory. "You have any more guns you plan on pointing at me tonight, prospect?"

"No, sir."

"Let him down," Garret said.

"Are you sure? He just tried to..." Ann's voice died down when she turned and saw Cory's sister's face full of tears.

"Please don't do this in front of Tiffany," Cory gasped out.

Ann clicked her lips and let go of him. "Why did you point a gun at us?"

"I thought you could have been with the cartel."

"So, you just open the door without confirming it? Are you actually developmentally disabled?" Garret shook his head with a sigh. "We're just here to ask you about what happened today. That's all, for now."

"I slipped out the back when that all popped off."

"We heard as much." Garret's eyes narrowed. He turned to Ann. "Take her somewhere else. We need to have a guy talk." His mouth contorted into a smirk.

"You're not going to hurt him?" Tiffany asked.

Garret looked over at her and gave a small smile. "Assuming he doesn't give me a reason to."

"That doesn't calm me down at all."

Ann pulled her along toward the staircase. "Why don't you show me your room, sweetie?"

Tiffany looked around Ann toward Cory.

"Go with her, Tiff." Cory nodded upstairs. "I'll be fine." He gulped and looked back at Garret.

"Okay." Tiffany followed Ann up the stairs and left the two men alone in the foyer.

"Now then," Garret finished watching the pair ascend and returned his focus back to Cory, "let's talk about exactly what happened today."

"I was in the back with Kelly."

"Doing what?"

"Cleaning, like Irving said to."

"Why was Kelly back there?" Garret asked.

"I don't know, sir. He was just back there, and we were talking. It made the whole thing more bearable, so I didn't question his motives. He was in a good mood and having guy talk, you know?"

"No, I don't know. Leave the questions to me." He took a step forward, further pinning Cory against the wall. "The bottom line is you left a brother to die. Do you realize that?"

"What?" Cory asked breathlessly.

"Irving, jackass!" Garret raised his voice with a pound on the drywall beside Cory's head. "You left an injured man to dodge lead all by himself. He could have died today because of your cowardice."

"What? All I did was try not to die, and you're getting on my case?"

Garret pushed him against the wall with his palm. "You've got balls I see. Not much brains, but you have guts to talk back right now. It's not my decision what happens to you. That's a club decision. I'm just here to bring you back. Of course, we'll take your darling little sister. We don't want those animals to get their hands on her while you're gone." He leaned in. "We don't leave people alone with them, unlike some people."

Cory looked away and said something under his breath.

"Speak up like a man. What did you say?" Garret jostled him.

"I panicked, alright? It was the first time I'd ever even heard a gun, much less had lead slung at me."

"Jesus Christ." Garret backed up a few steps. "Just stop talking right now if you know what's good for you."

Cory stared at the floorboards below.

"Now shut up and only answer my questions. Irving and Ronald said you escorted Kelly out the back. Is that much true?"

"Escorted is a bit strong."

"What does that mean?" Garret's tone got sterner.

"It means before I knew what was going on, Kelly got me on my feet and got us out of there. I wanted to go back in, but couldn't find a way without being filled full of lead. We ended up getting out of there, as opposed to sitting around all day. We thought they might have guys coming in the back."

"They didn't?"

"So far as we could see, no. They only came in the front entrance."

"That's odd." Garret scratched his chin. "Continuing on, how did you get here? Your bike was still at the clubhouse."

"Kelly dropped me off."

"Right. That makes sense. I guess we owe Kelly a little thanks for saving your worthless hide. At least he was trying to save one of us."

"As soon as the shots broke, he was moving. It was a little disconcerting watching a man act like a robot on impulse."

"That's called instinct, and if you survive a few more gun fights, you'll have that soon enough," Garret said. "Never mind that. Did you see what happened to Ronald?"

"He was the last one out the door, from what we saw."

"He came back after the cops left. Which means he was hanging around the local area. I assume your reason for not was to watch out for your sister up there?" Garret motioned up the stairwell.

"Yeah. I didn't want them to go after her, so I made my way back here."

Garret sighed. "Alright. Let's head back to the clubhouse and we can get this all straightened out. Bring a sleeping bag for the kid. You're probably staying over while we get this mess sorted out. I'll go get Ann and the kid." He scaled the stairs and looked back at Cory. "Hurry up." He pulled out his phone and hit the speed dial. "Come pick us up as soon as you can get free."

"We'll circle around. We're just getting some ice cream as we wait. The cop left a few minutes ago. I guess he didn't want to watch us eat, eh prospect?"

"No, sir," Garret heard Harold say.

"Yeah, whatever. Get over here. Oh, and get a cone for Cory's little sister. She'd like that." He hung up and reached the top of the stairs. He heard Ann's voice to his left. He walked over and stopped when he heard voices from a door immediately on his left. He knocked on the door. "We're ready." He backed up to the other side of the hallway and leaned back against the wall. "Pack an extra set of clothes. The kids are going on a sleepover."

"Do you have a backpack, honey?" Ann asked.

"It's over here." Rapid footsteps stopped and a sliding creak took over. Sounds of rustling cloth and a zipper filled the air.

"There we go. Your brother and you are going to be coming with us for a little sleepover."

"Cory said we had to stay inside tonight. It was dangerous."

"I know he did. He can't keep you both safe by himself though. Your brother relies on us, so you can too."

"Really?" the young female voice asked.

"Of course. That guy outside seems scary, but he's not. He's actually a big softie once you get to know him."

Garret cleared his throat. "I'm going to make sure Cory has got everything ready. Don't take too long in there." He descended the stairs and saw Cory lugging a huge green roll into the foyer before dropping it in front of the door. "We're about ready."

"At least you're quick about some things. The girls are on their way, and then we'll be off."

10

———

"That's all you have to say?" Richard slammed his palms down on the table in front of Cory.

Tiffany peeked around Ann's legs toward the table. She looked up at Ann and back to the table. She tugged on Ann's sleeve. She looked at her side to see Ronald and Harold.

Ann looked down and ruffled her hair. "Don't worry. Bosses usually chew someone out. He'll be fine." She smiled down at the girl. She returned her gaze toward the group of men across the room.

"Irv," Richard looked over at Irving across the table, "I'm putting it to you to mete out the punishment on this one. Don't go easy on him."

"Got it."

"Now get out while we figure out how to fix this shit."

"He means now." Tony pulled Cory's chair out. He yanked Cory up and pushed him toward the bar. He took the seat. "Anyway, what's the plan, boys?"

"Retaliation," Lucien said. "They tried to kill one of us for a third time." He glanced at Irving for a brief second.

"Not to break up this vengeance talk, but there's something everyone needs to be aware of. We need to head into the meeting room." Garret looked at every member sitting at the circular table. "It's confidential." He looked over at the growing crowd near the bar.

"Fine," Richard said. The entire group filed into the meeting room. Tony closed the two doors and locked it behind him before taking his seat. "What was so secretive that required this?"

Garret placed his folded arms onto the table in front of him and leaned forward. "When Ann and I found where their boss was, they got a phone call that we overheard outside the window. Someone warned them that we were on our way."

"You're not saying...?" Skuz asked.

"We have a rat, gentlemen," Garret said.

"You think Cory had a hand in this whole thing?" Irving asked.

"I don't know yet. That's what worried me." Garret pulled out his pack of cigarettes and squeezed it as he spoke. "I just know someone warned them ahead of time. Logic dictates they also told them when to strike at our weakest here."

"That rules out Irving and Harold then," Richard said. "They were here and nearly got shot."

"So were the other prospects, but that doesn't prove shit," Lucien said. "Ronald, Cory, and Kelly were in the back when it happened. Right?"

"Yep," Irving said, scratching his bald head. "Harold was up front polishing tables. Kelly parked out back and surprised us a bit. He had a good laugh at our expense."

"He's not involved in this." Richard shook his head. "Not after what he did to their higher up. Were they back there for any length of time before Kelly went back there?"

"Maybe five minutes," Irving said. "He hung around the bar, I got him a drink, and he said he was heading out. I heard him opening a door back there and talking. The next thing I knew, I was crawling for cover at the end of the bar."

"We have two prospects that had ample opportunity to make such calls," Lucien said.

"What do you propose we do?" Tony asked. "Torture them too? Dismiss them outright?"

"From now on, no more telling the prospects anything. If you catch them listening in, then we know they're too nosy for their own good. For now, Irving, you keep them too busy to do anything else. Get them to go to the fucking super-market for candy if you have to. Just keep them out of our business until we find out who exactly did this."

"Meanwhile, they've already moved their boss unless they're idiots." Garret tossed the pack onto the table. "We could go back there and question whoever we find, but I doubt they'll still be there. My bet is it's abandoned now."

"Maybe not," Richard said. "They didn't see you two, did they?"

"No. Why?"

"They might not have left then. It wouldn't hurt to check. Think about it. An unreliable asset gives you intel that someone's coming. No one shows up. What do you think? You'd think they're unreliable. Hell, you might even assume it's a trap to get you to move. I bet he's paranoid right now. This next trip won't just be a piddly two-person assault though. We're going balls deep the next time. Make sure you get your suppressors."

"Which means I have to leave my baby here." Garret frowned.

"You don't need that hand cannon everywhere." Skuz

elbowed Garret in the ribs. "Besides, size doesn't always matter the most."

"Yeah. If you're like Skuzzie here, you value stealth so she doesn't even know you were there," Irving said with a chuckle. "In his case, a small caliber works to his advantage."

Skuz swung his leg forward and connected with Irving's uninjured leg. "Stop fantasizing about my weapon already."

"How you two can joke at a time like this blows my mind." Richard cradled his head with an arm firmly planted on the table. "Cut it out until after the meeting."

The two stopped their antics and nodded.

"Now this has to go off without a hitch. The worst case is that nobody's there."

"Or it's a trap waiting on us," Lucien said. "They could boobytrap the place with explosives as they leave."

"Is there any way to avoid that if they did?" Skuz asked.

"We don't have or know any bomb disposal guys," Garret said. His eyes brightened and a smirk crossed his features. "I have an idea how we could minimize the risk. It's pretty crude though."

"Spit it out."

"We send one of the two prospects in question in first."

"What if they're not responsible?" Lucien asked, spittle flying out of his mouth. "We can't just assume they are. We'd be potentially killing an innocent man."

"Do you have any better ideas?"

"Tell them nothing," Tony said. "Send them home. If they still prepare for our arrival, then we know it wasn't them."

"That might actually work," Lucien said.

"It's better than just senselessly throwing one of our

innocent prospects into the grinder. Even if it would expose the rat, is it worth throwing the loyal one in with him?"

"No." Skuz shook his head.

"Besides, the best we can do is quarantine them in the back rooms," Garret said. "I kind of promised we'd keep the kid safe."

"Jesus Christ," Richard said. He gazed out the window at the little girl. "Yeah, you're right. We can't let that girl be put in danger because of us."

"Would it really be safe for her here if the other prospect is the traitor?" Lucien scratched the surface of the table with his index finger.

"I'll watch them both this time," Irving said. "Along with Harold, we can keep them in check."

"Good idea. We'll need everyone we have for this operation," Richard said. "You two will stay here with them. The rest of us will go see if their boss is still holed up in there. Everyone agreed?" He raised his hand above his head.

All but one at the table raised their hands in agreement.

"It's settled."

"Let me be the one to stay with Irv," Lucien grunted. "Send Harold. He could use the experience. I'll keep the other two in line."

Richard looked over toward the bar and the three prospects. "You sure?"

"If there's one thing I know how to do, it's to keep young men from doing anything stupid. You should know that."

"Ain't that the Lord's truth," Richard mumbled. "Fine. It looks like we're bringing along Harold, while the old man stays behind. You two stay safe back here. We'll leave here in the morning at four. Don't be late. I expect everyone to come packing. Make sure you have a suppressor." He glared at Garret. "We don't need every Tom, Dick, and Harry in the area code hearing us if shit goes south." He picked up the wooden hammer and slammed it onto the round wooden base. "Anything else before we go?"

"Who's staying here tonight? We need at least two," Garret said. "That is, unless you want a potential rat to stay here all night with that little girl."

"You invited them, didn't you?" Skuz asked. "Seems you should be the one to stay with them. Maybe you can get your girlfriend to stay with you and let us all sleep on our home beds."

Garret watched her pour a drink for Tiffany with a smile. "You might actually be right for once."

"Damn right I..." Skuz paused. "You dick, of course I am." He punched Garret in the shoulder.

"Meeting adjourned." Richard pushed his seat out and made for the door first. He flung it open and rubbed his eyes. He threw on his coat while the other men were still filing out of the room and left ahead of everyone else. "I'm heading home. Good night." He threw his hand up over his shoulder and shut the door behind him.

"Looks like I'm staying here tonight." Garret sidled over to Ann and the prospects.

Ann's hands dug into her hips. She shifted her weight to the side. "Why?"

Garret looked down at Tiffany hiding behind Ann's legs. "Someone's got to keep our newest guest safe tonight." He smiled down at her and back up at Ann. "Right?"

"Obviously."

"We need one more to stay tonight for safety's sake."

"I get it already," Ann said. "I'll stay too." Her right hand fell to her side and patted the girl's head. "We'll have them home by tomorrow I hope?"

"That's the plan," he squatted and got on eye level with

Tiffany, "so we can have you and your brother back in your own house." He looked up at Cory. "How's that sound, big brother?"

"Thank you, sir."

"Don't thank me yet because you're staying here too, along with Ronald."

"May I ask why?" Ronald asked from across the bar.

"No. You may not. For now, just worry about tonight. Why don't you start with making a few laps around the outside and reporting anything you see as suspicious?"

Tiffany moved over toward Cory and clinged onto his hand.

Ann yanked Ronald up and gave him a frown.

"Fine. You two stay inside. I'll go outside and look."

"Garret, why don't you accompany him?" Ann asked with a shining smile.

"Good idea." Garret got to his feet and walked toward the back entrance. "Prospect, since we're the ones left out in the cold, come talk with me as I walk. That is, unless you have better plans tonight."

"Of course not, sir." Ronald rushed to catch up to Garret.

"That leaves just us." Ann looked back over toward Cory and Tiffany. "Why don't we get your sleeping bag set up first, and then me and your brother can worry about everything else?"

Tiffany didn't verbally respond but merely nodded her head into her brother's arm.

"Okay then." She looked up at Cory. "Come on, big brother. Let's get her sleeping bag ready for the night."

Outside...

"Can I at least ask what's going on, sir?" Ronald asked.

"No, and if I were you, I'd keep my curiosity to myself until this dies down - if you know what's good for you." Garret kicked a stray pebble against the fence ahead. He turned the corner to his right. "Just keep a lookout for anything suspicious out here. You are packing, right?"

"Always."

"Good."

"This place looks completely different after dark," Ronald said.

"Most places do." Garret approached the front of the building. He heard assorted farewells along with the roar of many motorcycle engines. The deafening noise brought the conversation to a halt as the bikes filed out onto the pavement. Once the noise faded enough to hear each other, Garret nodded toward the entrance. "Yo, help me with this." He gripped the vertical metal bar and dug his heels into the pavement below to no avail.

Ronald took hold of the handle and the giant door slid closed.

Garret patted the metal and led the two away. "For what it's worth, I don't think you did it."

"Excuse me? Did what?"

"Nothing. Come on. Let's head out back and make sure that's still secure." He turned the corner around the clubhouse into the narrow alley. His left hand scraped the solid aluminum fence to his left with every step. "What did you think of today?"

"Are you asking if I'm going to bitch out and quit after today?" Ronald asked. "The answer's no. I knew what this life would entail before I signed up."

"Hmm," Garret grunted. "Does that look different to

you?" He pointed ahead toward the dumpster pushed against the back wall.

Ronald jogged up to the trash receptacle. "It looks like it's slightly out of position. Let me move it back." He circled around the dumpster and pressed his shoulder into it. He groaned in exertion as the giant brown stick pile inched its way closer to the visible hole in the fence. "This was probably my fault. I wasn't exactly in a hurry to block off Irving and Harold's only escape route."

"Is that right?" Garret asked, his face blank, his voice even. "You're quite the quick talker, aren't you?"

"You'd prefer I'd stutter and act like a fool? I can do that if you prefer."

"Stop. It's there." Garret walked up and stopped the sliding by force. He leaned to the side to look at the younger man. "Just keep your head down if you know what's good for you. Do everything Irving says."

"Why are you telling me the obvious, sir?"

"In my experience, you have to tell prospects a dozen times before they remember. I figure I may as well keep that tradition running strong. You'll need to know all these little complexities if you ever become a member. You may be given Irving's job to train the prospects after all."

"I guess that makes sense. I guess it beats going out on actual jobs like ya'll are tomorrow."

"What did you say?" Garret hurried forward and pinned Ronald against the wall.

"It was pretty obvious, sir. I don't know, nor want to know, where you're going; but whenever you all meet up you usually do."

Garret narrowed his eyes and stared deep into his eyes for a solid minute without blinking. He blinked and took a step backward. "I wonder about that."

"Sorry. I'm just a naturally curious person."

"It's known to kill cats. You should be careful with that quirk of yours. Especially in this line of work. Knowledge is a life and death affair; so don't overstep your bounds too quickly, or you may go the way of Icarus."

"Who's Icarus?"

"Are you a philistine? The guy who flew too close to the sun and his wax wings melted. Ring a bell? The point is, he grew too big for his britches too quickly. Learn from his mistakes, or else you may be doomed to repeat them."

"Alright then. I'll keep that in mind."

11

"Make sure not to talk to Ronald until this all settles down." Garret leaned forward and patted Harold's shoulder.

"You gave him a stern talking to last night?" Skuz asked from beside Garret. "I was expecting your girl here to be the one doing that."

"What exactly is that supposed to mean?" Ann leaned forward and glared at Skuz to her right.

"Stop messing around," Richard said. "Just remember the plan, and everything will go smoothly."

"We hope," Garret said from the back.

Tony poked his head above the back seat. "At least it's still dark out."

"It better be." Skuz covered his mouth as he let loose a massive yawn. "I didn't get up this early for nothing."

"Just in case, let's go over it one last time." Richard passed a large rolled up blue paper into the back.

Garret reached forward and unrolled it. He turned on the overhead light so everyone beside and behind him could see it.

"First Garret, Ann, and Skuz will be going in at point one."

Garret pointed to the big symbol marked one. "That essentially means we're going in the back for those who can't see back there."

"Tony and I are going in on the west side. That's marked by the big two."

Garret motioned toward the scribbled number.

"We'll text each other when we're in position, and then we sweep indoors. Remember, don't give any of them the benefit of the doubt. Wear your masks and gloves, and shoot first. When we're done, clean up after yourself. We'll clean out their upper echelon in one fell swoop if we do it right. The cops will believe it was just more gangland shootings."

"We're just going to leave the bodies there?" Harold asked. "That seems risky."

"Would you rather we take turns hauling what could be as many as six or seven bodies back to the van? That wouldn't exactly be subtle. We don't need to be quiet about this. In fact, we kind of want to be noticed. Just not so much that we end up the newest charter on the cell block. Understand?"

"Yes, Mr. President."

"Good."

"We'll set up a crossfire once we near each other in this room. If one of the two groups arrive early, set up a perimeter and hold it. They can't exit the building without going in one of these two rooms. It's to our advantage they're so narrow. It's a perfect kill funnel. Just don't be stupid and wander yourself into there. It works both ways, and I don't want to carry home any bodies today. Got it? Now everybody except me and the prospect put your masks and gloves on. I don't want any mistakes today."

Everyone in the van pulled out their respective masks and donned them, except the two in the front. They put on gloves before pulling out their respective firearms. "We're ready then." He pointed ahead out of the windshield. "Put us over there. There're numerous alleys we can make our way through without drawing attention. Once you let us out, head that way," his finger drifted to the right, "and let Garret's team out. When they're in position, park at the spot I told you. Keep the engine running and wait. That's all. You can do that, right?"

"I understand."

"Good. Now I don't want any more surprises," Richard said. "Let's make sure of it." He retrieved the phone from his pocket. "Eric, old friend, have you heard anything from our favorite group?"

"Nothing over here, guv," an undeniably Australian voice answered. "You lot are doing something then?"

"Nah, just wondering if you all had heard anything on the street."

"Only thing we've heard is some squabbles with the local dealers near them. They're apparently squeezing them hard. Some of the more prominent players are getting annoyed at the exorbitant fees they're charging to work. Have fun with whatever you're planning. Can we help?"

"We got this one. Next one though. We'll be calling on everyone you've got if it comes to it."

"Best of luck, Rich." The line went dead.

"We're good." Richard pocketed the phone. "By the way, prospect," he gripped Harold's shoulder, "if you leave without us," he squeezed hard, "you know what will happen. Right?"

"Garret would deal with me?"

"That's right," Garret said. "I'm tired and grumpy, and

you really don't want to piss me off tonight. Just remember, we'll be back before you know it. You leave, and you'd better disappear before we get back. Let's put it that way."

"Don't scare the boy so much," Skuz said. "He won't be going anywhere. He's my favorite prospect after all. Besides, he can just park a block away. He'll be safe from prying eyes. Just don't go too far. We still need to get out fast."

"We're nearly there." Harold pulled over to the side of the road and hit the brakes. "I'll park over there," he pointed to the left toward a walled off supermarket parking lot, "right near the street. Is that good?"

"That's perfect. No one will get suspicious if you're there, so relax," Skuz said. "Right, Rich?"

"Sure. Now let's get this done. Go down that street, and we'll unload Garret's team first." He pointed down a nearby side street.

Harold nodded and pulled back onto the street. "Good luck."

"Good luck to all of us, boys," Garret said.

"We're here," Richard said as the van screeched to a stop on an abandoned street beside the one Richard motioned to.

Ann flung the door open and jumped out along with Garret. Skuz jumped out of the opposite side. They closed the doors. As soon as they were closed they banged on the side of the doors, and the van took off onto the street.

"Let's get in position. Stay quiet and low," Garret said. The group followed him as they approached the compound. They snaked through the alleyways until Garret came to a stop in front of a low fence. "This is it." He got onto his tip toes. "There's the back door alright. I can see the fence we were on earlier."

"Now we just wait for Rich and Tony to get in position," Ann said. "Hopefully the old dude has still got it."

"You'd best watch it," Garret chuckled. "If he heard you say that, he'd flip his shit."

"I wouldn't worry about him," Skuz said, keeping watch on the road. "He's the one who taught most of us how to shoot and survive on the streets. If anything, I'm more worried about Tony."

"Talk about the guy who'd beat the hell out of you." Garret shook his head. "He'd cripple anyone who said that out loud. Now let's go make sure that door's open before they send their text."

"Sure, I'll cover you two back here so no one gets a jump on us." Skuz poked Ann's back as Garret peeked around the corner. He leaned in close. "You keep him safe."

"Come on. No one's out here." Garret hopped over the chain link fence and stalked forward. He reached the door and laid his hand on the knob. "It's unlocked."

"Must figure no one would be dumb enough to assault them," Ann whispered behind him.

They were interrupted with a whirring from Garret's pocket. He pulled it out and showed the screen to Ann.

"Go in ten seconds," was all the text said.

"Come on, Skuzzie," Ann called out in a low voice.

Garret's free hand was counting down with his other planted on the knob. "On me."

Skuz hurried over the fence and fell in behind Ann. "Got your back."

"Eight, nine, ten." Garret pushed the door in and readied his weapon into the empty, dark hallway ahead. He pushed forward and saw a doorway to his right. He turned and strafed, with his weapon at the ready. He saw a room with numerous tables lined with untold amounts of papers stacked high. He swiveled left and right as he entered the room. "It looks clear in here," he said with a low voice.

"The hallway was a dead end." Skuz entered the bigger room along with Ann. "I'll check over here on the left." He broke off from the group and moved toward the corner of the room with the biggest table.

"I'll check the right then." Ann went toward the smaller tables arranged near a white board.

"I'll make sure no one surprises you two." He moved directly forward into the room. A stairwell sat nestled into the far corner of the room heading upstairs. A noise to his right near the only other door caught his attention. He leveled his suppressed semiautomatic handgun over toward it as it burst open.

"Take it easy." Richard put up his hands when he saw it was Garret. "You scared the shit out of me, son." He lowered his hands. "We didn't find anyone on the way here. You?"

"Just a lot of papers so far. I was about to check the upstairs."

"Tony, go with him." Richard looked over toward Skuz and Ann. "I'm going to go see what intel I can find over there."

"Got it." Tony followed Garret up the stairs.

"Hold up." Garret held up his fist. "Do you hear that?"

A low whirring sound wafted down the stairs. Richard raised an eyebrow. "What is that racket?"

"We'd better find out." Garret creeped up the stairs, keeping his weapon at the ready.

"Right behind you." Tony stayed a step behind Garret.

"It's coming from up there." Garret looked toward the top of the stairs. "Sounds like from the left." He reached the top of the stairwell and pivoted left and right only to find no one. "Watch my back as I start trying to find that noise."

Tony turned his back to Garret and leveled his handgun down the hallway. He backstepped and stopped once he heard Garret a few steps behind him. "You just be careful on your side. I've got this one covered.

Garret pressed his ear against the nearest door. "Not this one." He moved further down the hallway and did the same to the next door. He nodded after hearing the noise, louder behind the wooden barrier. He sneaked over to Tony and tapped his shoulder. "They're over here. Now let's surprise them."

"Sounds like fun." He lined up on the opposite side of the door frame and looked over at Garret. "Ready."

Garret nodded. He reached out to the knob with his left hand and whispered. "One, two, three!" He pulled the door open, and they turned the corner.

Two men were inside facing the other way. The taller one with broad shoulders seemed to be watching the smaller of the two hovering over a paper shredder.

The taller spoke up. "Hurry up, man. I want to get out of here before anyone shows up."

"Too late. Now drop any weapons you have and stop what you're doing," Garret said.

"Is that what you think is going to happen?" the taller one asked.

"No sudden moves or we put you down," Tony said in a commanding voice. "Do not test me."

"Sorry, puto. I don't have a choice." Without warning the taller one wheeled around with an automatic machine pistol in his hands.

Muffled shots rang out from Garret and Tony's pistols,

and the man fell back onto the floor. He raised a shaky weapon up toward them, only to receive another volley of lead into his abdominal cavity. He fell backward and stopped moving.

"As for you," Garret moved his aim to the smaller man now cowering in the corner, "tell us what you're shredding there."

"Just what they told me to, man. Please don't shoot me. If I didn't do what they told me, they said they'd kill my family." He curled up into a ball and shook.

"Do you know where they went?"

"What?" the man asked. "Yeah, they told me where to meet up after I was done with this. Why?"

"You're coming with us. Don't worry, you'll be fine so long as you don't cause us any trouble. Grab the papers he was getting ready to shred." Garret stomped forward and roughly gripped his forearm. He yanked him into a standing position and dragged him out of the room and down the stairs.

"What was that racket? We'll have to leave now," Richard said.

"We have a few minutes," Garret said. He threw the small man forward onto the ground. "He knows where they are."

"Hello, friend." Skuz squatted in front of him. "We're going to be best friends."

"It's not like we found anything worth a damn down here. Fine, we'll take him along and question him. Let's get out of here before the cops show up."

"Is he our consolation prize?" Ann asked.

"Something like that."

"How can we be sure he knows anything?"

"I swear I do, miss." He raised his hands up to protect his head. "I'll tell you anything you want."

"I hate narcs like you." Ann delivered a sharp kick to the man's ribs. "Fine, let's get out of here then. Someone probably heard those shots. Shall I call our limo?"

"Go ahead," Richard said.

Ann walked off to the corner of the room and pulled out her phone. "Come pick us up now, and I mean now." She hung up and looked back at the group. "He's on his way."

"Then let's not leave him waiting," Richard said. Everyone get outside. Grab any intel you can. We may as well not let it go to waste to the police."

Everyone folded up any papers they could get their hands on and stuffed them into their pockets. A horn outside gave everyone pause, before they immediately made for the exit.

Garret reached down and grabbed one of the man's arms. "You're coming along."

Tony grabbed the other. "Don't even think of saying no." He and Garret dragged him out behind everyone else. The back doors flung open.

"Get in here, pussy." Skuz ushered the man inside.

He crawled inside, followed by Garret and Tony.

"Is everyone inside?" Richard asked from the front.

"Yep," Garret said. "Go."

"You heard him. Hit the gas," Richard said.

No sooner had those words been said then the van was moving forward onto the road.

"We're going to have some fun memories, you and me." Skuz licked his lips.

"You're my questioner?" he asked in a quivering voice.

"You wish," Skuz said. "I'd be gentle compared to him," he pointed to Garret, "if you know what I mean."

"Good God."

Ann peaked over the seats into the back. "My boyfriend's a lot of things. Gentle is not usually one of them. I'd recommend you not piss him off."

The man looked back at Garret, who was cracking his knuckles with a grin plastered on his face. "I hate liars. You're not a liar, right? The last guy was a liar."

"You should have seen it," Skuz said with a laugh. "He was begging all like 'Please don't rip my fingernails out.'" He descended into a howl of fake screams until Ann reached over the seat and slapped the back of his head. "Don't forget the ear lobes, if you're going to portray it badly. I specifically remember his cartilage getting stretched before it ripped with a wet snap."

"Oh yeah. How could I forget that?" Skuz asked. "Don't forget the cries as we buried him alive. That was a riot."

"Are you going to be as stubborn as the last guy?" Garret asked. "I learned a lot with the last guy. You want an example?"

The man stared blankly at him without nodding or shaking his head.

"You're the rude type, huh? Instead of what I did last time, I'll have to change it up with you. What do you think boss? What would suit a jackass like this?"

"Maybe this time you should cut off his hands entirely. He won't need those anymore if he doesn't speak."

"That's harsh, but I do have a saw I've been aching to try out." He flashed a smile. "Maybe after that I can try out my idea."

"You don't mean..." Tony trailed off.

"Yeah, I've always wanted to try plucking eyes out of a skull before. They always make it look so easy in the movies. I want to see what the fuss is about."

"I'll tell you anything you want. Just don't mutilate me."

"That's what we want to hear," Richard said. "We've got a questioning facility all set up for you."

Out in the Wilderness...

"Oh God. You're going to kill me either way, aren't you?" He fell forward thanks to a palm on his back pushing him out of the van.

"We're men of honor," Richard said. "Of course not. Just tell us what we want to know, and you get to go free. If not, well I'll let your imagination run wild." He circled around the van to the back with the rest of them. "Now let's take him to the facilities." He pointed off in the distance toward the tree line. "Tie him to the tree like the others."

Garret and Tony took an arm and dragged him toward the tree.

Skuz climbed out of the back and watched the three men walk off. "You think he actually knows anything?"

"Of course he does." Ann appeared from the other side of the van. "He was shredding evidence. Right?"

"That doesn't mean he knows shit," Richard said. "He could have just been the cleanup guy. Either way, he's not innocent. He was in there with one of their sicarios. He's connected in some way."

"It sounded like he's just a victim in all this to me," Lucien grunted as he jumped out onto the bare soil. "Didn't he say something about his family being killed if he says something?"

"That's if you believe him," Ann said. "Twig boys like

that are usually playing the weakling, trying to get sympathy."

"You base that off of anything?" Richard asked.

"I base that off seeing a white-collar looking dude in a gangster hideout. That shit doesn't happen naturally."

"Fair point. There's something off about him." Richard watched Garret pin the guy against the tree as Tony circled around it holding a long length of chain. "We'll have our answer by the end of the night. He doesn't look like the tough guy type. He'll fold before he's done drawing his knife."

"You want to bet on that?" Ann asked.

"Sure. Fifty bucks says he bitches out before he even lays a finger on him."

"I'll take that bet." Ann reached forward and grabbed his hand with a shake."

"What about you? You want in on this?" Richard asked Skuz.

"I don't want to take your money. It wouldn't be proper." He winked toward Ann. "Sorry, but there's something wrong with that dude. He's not all that he appears. Everyone keep your eyes on him."

"What do you know?" Richard asked. "You must be getting dementia. He's a limp noodle if I ever saw one."

"Is that what you see, or what you hope? Be careful now. Don't confuse the two. That's when mistakes happen, and when that happens..."

"People die. I've heard this dozens of times. I know already. I just think the guy's a wimp. I'm not underestimating anything here."

"I hope you're right."

"Now let's go watch the show. It looks like it's about to begin." He walked toward the tree line along with the rest of

the gang. They approached the pair making the last adjust-
ments to the chain. "Are we about ready?"

"There we go," Tony said. "It's tied. There's no way he's
moving now."

"Good. Now it's my turn. I'll be right back. I just have to
go get my tools. Don't go anywhere now."

"Don't forget the screwdriver," Skuz said. "I keep telling
you that'd be the best way of taking an eye out. Just jam it in
there, twist it, and pluck it out."

"Nah, you need something with more of a scoop shape
for a clean removal," Ann said.

"Who said I wanted it to be clean?"

"Fair enough."

"Let's start this now before he gets back." Richard took a
step forward. "If you answer now, this will go easier for you.
So, where are they?"

"What?"

"You know we're not playing, right? You will be blind by
the end of the night and be unable to eat if you keep this
tough guy shit up? Where are they?" He pounded his fist
into the wood beside his head.

"I was just hired to shred their documents in there.
That's all, man. I swear." He yanked against the chains
around his waist. His hands at his sides opened and balled
into fists. "I don't know anything else. They stuck my wife's
cousin with me. He's a big dude and he had a gun. He told
me what to do. They gave me a quick three thousand bucks,
along with a threat to my family if I said anything."

"Sounds like it's already too late for that, since you've
already told us. You may as well put your trust in us taking
care of them for you. Where are they?"

Garret gently pushed Skuz to the side and dropped the

red toolbox with a loud clatter. "How's it going, boys? Is he talking?"

"I don't know," Richard said, taking a step toward the imprisoned man. "Are you?"

"All I can tell you is the address they gave me to meet back up with them afterward. I don't know where their base of operations is. I'm just a hired hand."

"Are you a cleaner?" Garret kneeled and opened the toolbox. "There's no way they hired some random guy." He grabbed a screwdriver out of the box and stood up.

"A cleaner? I'm just a janitor. My wife's cousin needed a favor. When I showed up, they threw me in a van and hauled me over there. As soon as we got there, he pushed me upstairs and ordered me to dispose of everything. You know everything from there."

"Their rank and file are even disposable to them?" Richard asked. "They had to have had an inkling we'd be on our way."

"They used their own family for their own ends?" Skuz asked.

"Damn." Ann shook her head. "They're more ruthless than I imagined."

"We all have indiscretions." Garret rested the flat head against the tied-up man's forehead. "Now tell us the address, and we let you go. You haven't seen our faces yet. We have nothing against you. Just don't tell anyone anything that happened tonight, and you're home free. It's a pretty sweet deal, right? Don't fuck it up for yourself by trying to be brave. They won't thank you for your service, while we will. Make the right decision." He applied more pressure onto the screwdriver.

"Alright, man. Just don't take my eyes. I need them to provide for my family."

Richard stepped forward and rested a hand on Garret's arm, lowering it. "What's the address?"

"Alright already. It's a little place off Highway nineteen. It's just off Amado."

"That's not too far east of here," Tony said. "Where exactly is it?"

"It's on Amado Montosa road. Just look for the place with a bunch of cars parked in a circle. That's all they said."

"I know where that is."

"That went a lot easier than I expected," Richard said. He held out an upside palm to Skuz. "Pay up, young man."

"He shoved that screwdriver against his head. That was against the bet."

"He never laid a finger on him. Technically it was my win, and you know it."

Skuz grumbled and dug around in his pocket, before laying a few bills into Richard's grasp. "What should we do with the coward now?" He looked back at their prisoner.

"I thought you were letting me go? I don't know who you are, and I don't want to know. I'll just disappear, and you'll never hear from me again, man."

"We did promise we'd let him go." Garret turned back to the group. "He could come in handy later."

"I'll do whatever you want. Just don't blind or kill me," the man begged. Tears rolled down his eyes and he sniffled between words. "I have a family."

"Shut up when we're talking," Richard said. He snapped his fingers. "I'll tell you what. You give us your phone number and address, and we'll let you go. We need to make sure you hold up your end of the deal. That's all."

"Okay, man. Sure."

"Get him down and get his information. We'll drop him off first, and then decide what to do with this."

Garret turned back to him. "You're lucky. You were the first smart contestant we ever had."

Tony circled around the tree with a laugh. "I am a little disappointed we didn't get another show though. The last guy was great entertainment, but not nearly as helpful."

Ann stepped forward and traced the man's jaw with her index finger. "I can't tell if you're a good man or just a coward. Either way, I have to respect the family man persona you're outputting here."

"Don't even think of running, or we'll shoot," Tony said before the chains went slack and then fell.

"He's smarter than that." Skuz stepped forward and stood beside him. He threw an arm around his shoulders. "At least he seems smarter than that so far. You wouldn't want to piss me off, would you?"

"No, sir."

"At least he knows how to show respect, unlike some of you."

"Like you deserve it." Garret grinned and playfully shoved Skuz away with a chuckle. He took their captive's arm and dragged him back to the van. "I sure don't envy the conversation you're going to have tonight with the wife."

"Ooh, you're right," Skuz said. "We did kind of kill her cousin, didn't we? If we don't kill you, she sure will. Maybe it'd have been nicer if we had killed you," he cackled as Garret dragged him away toward the van.

"Oh, I hadn't even thought of that. She's going to blow a gasket." His head hung down.

"If I were you, I'd tell her to be thankful she didn't lose her husband too. That's about the only silver lining for her. Don't try to rationalize it. She'll just get pissy. Don't blame him either. She won't want to hear it."

"Why are you helping me?"

"I'm not. I'm just speaking out loud about what I'd do. Don't get it twisted. Or you could hide it, and hope she doesn't pin it on you when she finds out he's dead. I don't really care what you do." He pushed him up into the back of the van. "Now don't get any cute ideas. Just stay there and be a good boy. Just in case you get any weird ideas about stealing this van, don't forget that we know where you live. Turn around really quick."

The man did so.

Garret reached into his back pocket and took out his wallet. "As an insurance policy, remember we know where you live. As an additional safety net, turn around." He grabbed his arm and flipped him around. He reached inside the van and grabbed the rope on the side. "No hard feelings." He set to tying his hands together behind his back. "Now be good." He slammed the doors shut and walked back to the group.

"Are we really sending him back to his family?" Lucien asked Richard.

"Why not? He might have an inkling who we are, but no proof. Besides, he owes us one. We could use him later to our advantage."

"If we want to capitalize on the intel, we should go tonight," Ann said. She raised her hands up in a placating manner once all eyes turned to her. "I know I'm not a member, but they could be doing a mobile command center thing. They could be set to leave that address at six in the morning. We don't know. I'm just throwing it out there."

"She could be right." Garret approached and stopped between Ann and Richard. "If they're panicking, like I think they are, they'd be moving as much as they can. This might be our only chance to hit them unexpectedly."

"They've stayed one step ahead of us so far, Pres," Tony

said while tapping his foot on the soil. "This is our chance to catch up and end this once and for all."

"We could use him, if you're really worried." Lucien pointed toward the van. "I wouldn't trust his acting skills, but if you really wanted to test the waters, it's an option. Just send him in with his phone on, and we'll get all the intel we want."

"We save his ass only to send him back to the wolves?" Richard asked. "I like it. He could prove useful."

"So, we're not sending him back to his family until after this spying debacle?" Garret asked. "Because we're probably not going to get him back after we send him to his wife. My bet is the guy bolts in the middle of the night with his family, if we send him back."

"We have no loyalty to him," Skuz grunted. "He's been helpful, but he's not one of us. I say we go for it. What's the worst that happens? He dies? So what?"

"That's a nasty business, but not like we haven't done it before. Right, Garret?"

Garret leaned away from everyone and spat onto the ground. "Don't remind me of that business. I had to watch that poor bastard get shanked like a pig. I liked that dude too."

"It had to be done."

"For the good of the club. I know." Garret grimaced. "I still don't have to like it though. Having said that, I vote we use him. I don't care about that guy. He might be helpful now, but there's no guarantee he'll stay that way. My bet is as soon as he gets inside, he'll rat us out to the cartel. We need a plan for if that happens."

"Fair enough," Richard said. "Cowards rarely find their courage, much less for those blackmailing them."

"We could force his loyalty if we send a few people to his

wife's home," Skuz said. "Pull what we did with Yeltzin. It worked then, and it'll probably work here. We could send Tony over there. He could handle it. You could pretend to be the bearer of bad news and stick around there while this goes down."

"They'd never let me in. It's too late at night. All I'd get is either shot through the door, or the police called for trespassing. Besides, we don't even know the family. It wouldn't work here."

"Which just leaves planning for the betrayal on the site," Richard said. "We could have everyone stationed around the place at different locations. If it goes sideways, we'd have them surrounded. But we'd be spread thin."

"That," Garret said, "or we could rig something up to take them all out. We don't need explosives. All we need is something to put into their ventilation. It'd flush them outside, where we'd be waiting with guns drawn. All we need is the right chemical introduced into their ventilation system."

"We do have some gasoline in the back of the van, but that wouldn't help too much," Tony said. "They'd smell it as soon as we introduced it."

"Maybe, but we do have some antifreeze," Ann said. "All we'd need is to aerosolize it and we'd be golden. They probably wouldn't pass out right off the bat, but it would affect their hand/eye coordination and vision. And, it could possibly knock them out."

"How do you even aerosolize anti-freeze?" Skuz asked.

"How do you aerosolize anything? You dump it into the building through the vents."

"I don't think that's how that works," Tony said. "However, it would cause a panic. If we could get one person upstairs with gasoline and dump it into the system via the ducts, they'd be forced to leave the building for fear of death."

"Right into our waiting hands," Richard said. "We'll figure it out on site. Everybody load up. We're on the warpath tonight."

12

_____

"One problem's solved, and another one reveals itself." Garret sighed, staring out the window at the building they were directed to. "They have patrols going around the building, and there's no ladder leading to the roof. They must have one in that shack out back"

"The patrols won't be a problem," Richard said. "We'll take them out quietly, and let you climb up to flush them out. Still, it'd be better if you didn't go alone."

"I'm going with him," Skuz said.

"You wish you were as quiet as me," Ann said. "I'll go."

"Bitch, you're six feet tall. You're as stealthy as a basketball player slinking around. I'm going."

"Both of you shut up," Richard said. "G, who do you want with you for this? You're the one going. It's your choice."

Garret looked between his best friend and his girlfriend. He raised a finger toward Ann. "Sorry, buddy. You're not exactly the quiet type."

"Fine, then I'm taking the rifle and watching your ass. Don't even try and stop me." He climbed over the backseat past everyone. He flopped on the cabin floor next to their captive. "How are you doing?" He grabbed the long rectangular box and opened it, revealing the gun parts inside. "Don't mind me."

"I guess that's settled then," Richard said. "T, Harold, and I will split up. We'll cover the entrances for when they come running out. Remember, we fire as soon as we have confirmation they're ES-15. No shooting unidentified targets. It never ends well for anyone. Garret, when you two are done, let us know with a text before you start your thing up there."

"Just to throw it out there, they may not move." Ann stopped Garret's departure with her words.

"What the hell's that mean?"

"It means if they're asleep, they won't smell it. It may just kill them in their beds. That's best case, but it is an option."

"When have we ever been so lucky?" Richard asked. "Plan for them to be pissed."

A click along with a laugh came from the back. "Don't bump me, or I'll stab you. Got it?"

"Get your ass up here," Richard said. "I don't want you anywhere near him when he's shooting. Just keep your head down, and you'll be fine."

Tony reached into the back and dragged their prisoner into the front cabin. He threw him onto the cabin floor between his legs and left him there.

"Whenever G's ready, we'll head out. He and his girl will head upstairs. While they're doing that, we'll all get in position. Our guest will piss his pants right where he is, and everyone gets to go home tonight. Clear?"

Everyone nodded without a word.

"Good. As for the guards patrolling, we'll need to deal with them quietly. Ideas?"

"We're not in any big hurry, right?" Garret asked. "I have an idea, but it may take a little while."

"Shoot."

"This place has plenty of cover around. They seem to be patrolling around the house every ten minutes or so. We'll get to cover near the house. Once they're on this side, we'll take them out with hand-to-hand combat. It's quieter than shooting anyway. With any luck, no one will hear them hit the ground."

"It sounds like it'll work. If anything does go wrong, everyone cover them. Don't get too close before they do this. We don't want anyone caught with their pants down away from the group."

"Let's do this before we freeze to death or they circle around. I don't want to wait another ten minutes."

"Agreed," Richard said. "They just passed. We should have time to get into position. Stay low, quiet, and keep your aim steady. If we do this right, this war is over. Don't mess this up, and don't get yourselves killed - or you'll answer to me."

Garret leaned over and whispered in Ann's ear. "Ready?"

"Always."

"We're on our way," Garret said, throwing the van's sliding door open. He held the door open for Ann before sliding it closed, with care not to make any noise.

"Let's head this way." Ann pointed ahead, toward the building near a thicket of trees. "It has more cover." She took the lead, leaving Garret behind. "Come on."

Garret followed behind and took cover behind a nearby tree. He peeked around the wooden obstacle and saw no dancing flashlights nearby. "We can make it now."

"We'll wait. I'm not taking chances. Why? Is the big man

cold? Besides," her smile faded, "we need to take them out for the rest of the boys."

Garret's ears perked up and he raised a lone index finger to his lips. He pointed around the tree.

She gave him the okay sign with her fingers, then bent down and picked up a large rock. Garret followed her lead and waited behind the cover as flashlights appeared on the ground near the corner of the house, along with quiet voices speaking Spanish.

Garret took out his knife with his left hand and gripped it tight. The voices grew louder until they were right behind him. He heard the flick of a lighter along with a loud exhale.

"Now's our cue," Ann whispered.

Garret peeked around his cover to see the two men about ten feet away, facing the house, smoking cigarettes. "I've got the right one."

"Fine with me."

Ann emerged from cover at the same moment Garret did. The two tossed their rocks against the house as they approached. The rocks bounced off the bricks. The men tensed up and moved to investigate the walls.

Ann lunged forward with unnatural speed and tackled the one on the left, while Garret took off into a dead heat toward his target. He wrapped his arms around his target's neck and squeezed. "Just go to sleep. It's for your own good." He wrestled with the struggling man's errant hands. "Fine, you asked for it." He transferred the knife into his right hand and held it against his captive's throat. "Stop," he growled into his ear.

The man ceased struggling in his grasp.

"Good, we're backing up now." He looked over at Ann who was laying on top of her target's back. Her target was already limp and unmoving under her. He backpedaled with the man back behind cover. "Thanks for cooperating. Here's your reward." He stuck the blade deep into his throat and sliced horizontally. A spurt of blood shot out of his neck. The man brought his hands up to the wound to stem the bleeding, but within ten seconds he was on the soil face down in a puddle of his own blood. Garrett leaned around the cover and saw the coast was clear before returning to his original position beside Ann. "Now to just get the ladder with the same efficiency, and we're in the clear." He led the pair around the house and stopped with his back to the wall. He leaned around the corner. "The coast is clear." He turned the corner and ran to the shed. "Lucky for us, they didn't lock it." He grabbed the handles and pulled them open.

Ann ducked inside. "Found one and some gas." She hopped back outside. "Now close that, and let's get this show on the road." She led the two back around the corner and set up the ladder. "I'll go first. Cover me." She climbed up the rungs and onto the roof. She peeked her head over the side. "You're next."

Garret leaned down, grabbed the gas can, and climbed up. He set aside the gas can and lifted the ladder up onto the roof before gently laying it down beside them. "Phase one complete. Now it's time to let everyone know we're in position." He pulled out his phone and texted. "Done."

"Let's wake them up with a gas scare then." She hoisted the gasoline canister up and dragged it over to the exposed ventilation shaft nearby.

"Wait a minute." Garret's hushed voice stopped her in her tracks.

Spanish speaking voices were below them where they had climbed up. They both froze as the pair below carried on their conversation. "Aqui?"

"Si."

"No veo nada. Vamanos." The pair below continued off and turned the corner.

Garret lowered the ladder back down to the ground below and nodded over to Ann.

Ann poured the gasoline down the ventilation shaft, holding it upside down as the fuel sloshed down the shaft. She tossed the can down and stalked over to Garret once it was empty.

"Ladies first."

Ann descended onto the top rung of the ladder. "What a gentleman." She reached into her belt halfway down the ladder and brought out her pistol. She sprinted off toward the nearest tree and took cover behind it. She raised a hand up and gestured Garret over with her index finger.

He got halfway down the ladder when loud slams and screams came from inside. He hopped off the ladder and hurried toward the tree line near Ann. He whipped out his .357.

"I thought you left that at the clubhouse."

"Never." Garret brought the barrel of his revolver to his lips and kissed it. "This baby has kept me alive. I'm not leaving her behind."

"Her?"

"Well, it's not a dude."

"Jesus," Ann said. "Here they come."

Shots rang out from the other side of the building. "Sounds like the party's starting," Garret said. He leaned against the tree and raised his revolver toward the left side of the building. "You watch the right side. They'll be running once they realize that side's a bust."

"Right." She leveled her gun toward the other side of the building.

Garret squeezed off two rounds as figures circled around the building in a run. They fell forward, clutching their chest.

Ann fired off a round. "Damn." The window shattered next to the man she'd aimed at, raining glass shards down onto her target's back. She fired off another round, this time putting him down.

"Do you smell smoke?" Garret asked.

"All the shots going inside must have caused a spark."

"At least that'll make the clean-up easier." He fired off another round. "They just keep coming out of the woodwork."

"That tends to happen when it's on fire," Ann shouted over the blaring cracks of the gunshots echoing around them. "Just how many do you think there are?" She ducked behind the wooden cover and ejected the magazine before inserting a new one and ratcheting the chamber. She brought her arm around her cover and leveled it at her side of the building when the shots stopped ringing out. Her eyes never left her side. "You think they're all dead?"

"Don't know. They could be waiting inside thinking the gasoline is better than out here, especially if the boss is in there. We'll need to find out definitively before we go. I'm not looking forward to that."

"Or we could just burn it to the ground, after dragging the bodies inside and barring the doors shut."

Garret's face lit up. "I like the way you think. It'd save on cleaning, kill them all, and get us home faster."

"I'm just a regular genius. All we'll need is something to block the two doors, and we're golden."

"Watch my back." Garret stepped out of the wooden cover and inched toward the building. He turned the tall ladder into a small ladder by collapsing it down and folding it until it was the height of the doorknob. He propped it under the knob. "That's one down." He pulled out his phone and hit a single button. "Rich, find a way to brace your door shut. We'll burn it down. If anyone's still inside, they'll barbecue alive. It'd save us the time and danger of going in and hunting them down."

"Good idea. We'll bar this side. You got the matches?"

"Always, but it's already aflame. Smell that smoke?"

"Then toss a match in to be safe when I text you next." A click sounded in his ears. He reached into his back pocket and took out the book of matches. He tucked the gun down the front of his belt and struck a match against the back of the book, eliciting a small flame from the reddened end. His pocket rumbled. He used his free hand to dig out his gun and shoot the nearby window before tossing the flame inside. More smoke billowed out of the building inside of fifteen seconds. He made a break back toward cover and watched. "They'll come out now, or they're dead."

"How long will we stay here? That smoke will give this place away soon. I'd say we have fifteen minutes tops before fire fighters start arriving on scene."

"Plenty of time. We'll be out inside of five. Either they stay in there and die, or we shoot them. Either way, it'll be quick."

"Let's just hope it spreads outside a little. Those bodies are going to be a problem if it doesn't."

"Then help me fix it really quick." He made his way over to the bodies. "You grab yours and follow my lead." He hefted them over his shoulder and tossed them into the shattered window.

She grunted in exertion and lifted her victim over her shoulder before doing the same. "At least that's one more problem taken care of." She rubbed her shoulder. "I need to do laundry tonight. Our clothes are a mess, as usual."

"You say the most mundane things at extraordinary times. You know that?"

"Girls just don't like other men's blood all over their clothes. I assumed it was the same for you."

"I go through a lot of shoes, but never really thought of much else." His pants pocket vibrated, and he pulled out his phone. "Yeah?"

"We're out of here. Get back to the van. We have some news."

"We're pulling out? Are we sure everyone inside is taken care of?" Garret glanced back at the quickly escalating inferno in front of him.

"Oh, we're sure alright," Richard's glum voice answered. "We have another situation here."

"Why am I not surprised?" Garret asked. "Fine, we're on our way."

"What was that about?" Ann asked.

Garret pocketed the phone. "We're leaving. Apparently Richard will explain on the road." He placed a hand on her back and guided her back to the group. "Who knows what surprise awaits next?"

On the road a few minutes later...

"What was the big hurry?" Garret asked. "Why did you sound so out of breath?"

Richard turned off the radio with a twist and peered around his seat toward the back. "We were half right."

"So, are we returning this dude like we said?" Garret

jabbed a finger over his shoulder toward the bound man who had been returned to the back compartment. "He did tell us where they were."

"Yeah, we're on our way now. The problem is, we were only half right, like I said. I have no doubt that our source back there told us everything he knew. What I didn't imagine was his giving him that address."

"What are you getting at?"

"That wasn't their headquarters."

"Wait," Skuz said. "What are you saying? Who the hell did we just torch?"

"Didn't you notice the lack of males?" Lucien grunted. "It was all women."

"Not on our side," Ann said. "We saw two guys with guns who were pissed off."

"She's right," Garret said. "We only saw men."

"How nice for your conscience," Richard said with heavy sarcasm lacing his words. "For us, it just went by too fast. Once the dust settled, we noticed. We checked one of their wallets and got a name. We need to find out who she was. She could have been one of the higher up's lady."

"Why would he give a little pencil neck like him the address to where his family was staying?" Garret asked with a shake of his head. "It doesn't make full sense to me."

"He probably figured his muscle head bodyguard wasn't going to bite the dust," Skuz shrugged. "He guessed wrong."

"We're assuming the worst right now," Richard said. "I'm not letting another member get wounded due to this. We're all staying at the club tonight. This time we're not going outside, we're having our watch inside. No more getting sniped. They've proven they won't stop at anything to get at us. Let's not make it easy for them."

"Couldn't they just send another attack helicopter after us?" Skuz raised his hand.

"Yeah," Richard said in a glum tone. "They could. I'm hoping they blew their influence and money with the last one though. Otherwise, we're fucked."

"If we did just kill the boss's family, hell is about to rain down," Tony said. "What we've seen so far will pale in comparison."

"We've seen the worst they have," Garret said. "We've survived it, and we will again. Let's just get this idiot back to his family so they can run for their life. Because after that, my bet is that anyone who knew about that place will be purged."

"Especially if that really was the missus," Tony said. "There were three guys there, but you should have seen our side."

"Yeah," Skuz said. "One guy with a gun came first, then the next thing we saw was a woman on fire inside the window banging against the glass, screaming. She beat on that surface like a madwoman, but eventually the fire engulfed her in front of our eyes."

"Damn," Ann said. "We only saw guys on our side of the house. It's sounding more and more like a family hot spot for ES-15 north of the border. Which means this war just got hotter than ever."

"I'll call the Outback Boys. We're going to need all the help we can get from this point on. I don't care what the payback we're going to owe. I want them involved in every operation from here on out. We're going to need the manpower now. We'll figure out the payment details later, but we need their backup now."

"Good idea," Garret said. "We still have those emp

grenades and I know at least one of them is hungering to try them out."

"Come to think of it," Tony said, "if we'd used those, maybe this wouldn't have been so bloody."

"Nah, it'd been just as bloody," Garret said. "It would have just been much harder. Don't start second guessing yourself now."

"Right. I'll just try and forget those vivid memories. She was looking right at me."

"She made her bed when she got involved with them," Richard said. "Don't feel bad for them. She was probably every bit the bitch her husband is. Power tripping isn't limited to the boss in my experience. Sometimes the little lady can be just as powerful in her own right. We still made major progress tonight. If nothing else, we've pissed them off majorly."

"Is that really an accomplishment though?" Harold asked. The van went silent. "I mean, what does that gain us?"

"Shut up, prospect," Garret said. "We know what we're doing here. We struck a blow they won't recover easily from. They'll make more mistakes now, and that is how we'll win."

13

"Did you see how fast that guy ran inside?" Skuz asked with a laugh. "I bet they're already out of town."

"That's if he's smart," Tony said.

"What is that?" Garret leaned forward between the driver and passenger seat. "Is that smoke?" He placed a hand on Harold's shoulder. "Slow down and park far away."

Harold turned onto the street where the clubhouse was located and pulled to the side of the street. He put it into park and stared ahead at the scene.

Fire trucks surrounded the building as billowing clouds of smoke reached up into the night sky.

"I guess we know who did this," Garret muttered in a somber voice.

"Goddamned ES-15," Richard growled through gritted teeth."

Skuz immediately pulled out his phone. "Irv? Where are you, Lucian, and the other prospects?"

"I don't know about them, but they dropped me off at home an hour ago. Why?"

"Someone burned our clubhouse down."

"What?" Irving's loud voice asked.

"Yeah, man. I'll tell you more later, but I just wanted to be sure you were alright."

"Yeah, I'm fine. You want me to check on Lucian and the prospects?"

"Let me check." Skuz placed his palm on the phone's bottom. "Rich, should we check on Lucian and the two other prospects? Irv says he's home and fine."

"Forget the prospects for now. We need to end this war, and I mean now. For tonight, we need to pick up Lucian and find a place to stay."

"We can set up revolving watches at my apartment, but it'll be a bit cramped," Garret said. "If we keep three men patrolling outside and one stationed at the door, we should be safe."

"For how long?" Skuz asked. "A day? We still are going to have a horde of police asking questions about this fire tomorrow. They'll be following us for a week at least."

"Then we'll just have to deal with it," Richard said in a gruff fashion. "I'm not letting this go unanswered." He pulled out his own cell phone and dialed. "We are ending this tomorrow. There's no more of this shit. I'm making sure of it." He paused for a second. "Yeah, Eric? I need a favor. We'll talk tomorrow morning. Just make sure you're available. Try and get any intel on our favorite group's location. I don't care what you have to do. I'll pay one and a half times the usual. Just get it done please. I'll owe you one."

"Sure, buddy. I'll put out all the feelers. If they're in the state, we'll find them. By the way, I saw on the news about your club house. Sorry about that, man. They really have no honor."

"Yeah. Thanks for this."

"I'll even send some muscle with you tomorrow if you'd

like. Did your injured mate get out of there before the fire started?"

"Irving's home safe for now. We're going to pick him and Lucian up first and then lay low tonight."

"Good idea," Eric said. "It seems like you've really set them off this time. Be careful out there."

"You too." Richard hung up the phone. "There. By tomorrow we'll have our intel and we'll be able to end this." He looked over at Harold. "Take us to Irving's and then to Garret's."

The van pulled out onto the road and passed by the burning club house. Every man near the right window gazed out at the building. Assorted emotions crossed their faces. Rich's was a transparent mask of rage, while Tony shook his head with a long face.

"We can always rebuild." Richard's even voice broke the silence. "A building ain't shit in the grand scheme of things. It can be replaced with money. Inside of a month we'll have the money if this all goes well. Add another three for the construction, and this attack of theirs means nothing. Anyone have any ideas for when we find where they are?"

"I say we bring a lot of gasoline, lots of locks, and some matches," Skuz said. "Lock them in the place, spread gasoline in the middle of the night, and then this time we just torch the whole fucking thing with them inside."

"A good idea," Garret said. "We could also just go simple and douse them in a torrent of bullets. That's always fun."

"Too loud," Tony said. "I say we get unconventional."

"I like the sound of that." Richard smiled and looked back. "Do go on."

"You know how there's that DDC building around here, right?"

"The Disease Destroying Control?" Ann asked. "What about them?"

"I know a guy who works there on some heinous shit. We could buy some of it, toss it inside the place, and then lock them inside."

"Too risky, but I like the idea," Richard said. "We might get infected. Though I do admit the idea of el Jefe getting infected with a blight on mankind does tickle the cockles of my heart."

"Just floating ideas. I helped that dude out with a love problem in high school, so he owes me one. Just let me know if you need it."

"No need to get too exotic in your methods," Ann said, a smirk painting her features. "We just want them dead with no questions asked. Right?"

"Go on," Skuz urged.

"We get some carbon monoxide. Pump it inside while they're asleep, and they'll never wake up. The authorities will just think it was a leak. Bonus points since we won't be shot at again if we do it right. We just need a source of the stuff first."

"That's assuming they don't have an alarm system in place," Richard said.

Ann crossed her arms. "You could always have a backup plan, like shooting them in the face if they do run out."

"That's not quite as easy to explain or clean up," Richard said. "I do like the disease play."

"I vote for it," Garret said.

"Me too," Skuz said.

"It's better than us going up in there in a fire fight," Tony said. "I vote for it."

"That makes four votes. Tony, call the dude and set it up. We need a disease that's slow killing. These jackasses are staying a step ahead of us. We need to give up on catching him directly. We'll use his own henchmen against him. They'll infect him for us if we pull this off. Just have him grab something nondescript. We don't need people getting wind of this. That place has fire escapes, right?

"I think so. Why? Are we making a pickup?"

"We're not asking him to smuggle it out. If he gets caught, we're fucked. Have him call us when he's got it all set up. We'll swoop in, grab the box, and deliver it to the place. The shooting all of them plan is our backup."

"Sounds like a plan," Garret said.

"We're set then."

Harold slowed the van and parked by the sidewalk. "I'll go get Irving then?"

"Take it easy, prospect." Garret slid open the back door. "We'll go get him." He grabbed Skuz by the coat arm and dragged him out of his seat. "You're with me."

"It's midnight," Skuz groaned. "You think his family will mind if two guys in full colors walk up and ring the doorbell?"

"If they do, who cares? I don't care what they think." Garret climbed the stairs and bashed his index finger onto the doorbell button.

"Oh sure. What's not to worry about an angry mother or father? I hear they're great to converse with, especially when you're the source of their disapproval."

"What the hell do you want?" A gruff male voice asked. The barrel of a shotgun poked through the crack in the open door.

Garret stared down the darkness of the barrel. "We're here to pick up your son. We called him a few minutes ago. Go ahead, ask him."

"You're those hooligans?" he asked. The door opened

fully to reveal a doddering old man. His thinning gray hair sat atop his head. His eyes narrowed as he looked down at Garret and Skuz's attire. "He's fine, no thanks to you. He's not going anywhere with you. You got him shot in the first place."

Garret raised both his hands above his head. "Look, sir. We don't want any trouble. As far as we're concerned, he's part of our family. We want no blood here. We're here because he's in danger sitting here alone and injured with no defense but an old man with a rusty rifle."

"You got sack. I'll give you that." The old man glanced over Garret's shoulder. "How many are in there?" He pointed with the tip of his rifle.

"Four more," Garret said.

"What about you?" The old man turned his attention to Skuz's purple hair. "What the hell happened to you, boy? You look ridiculous."

"It's just my style. Can you put that down now?" Skuz glanced down at the shotgun.

The old man lowered the barrel but did not holster the weapon. "Irv!" he yelled. "Your gang is here. Get over here." His eyes never left the two.

Garret peered over the old man's shoulder and saw Irving hobbling into view from the upstairs hallway. He got to the stairs and carefully descended. "Dad, please put the gun away. These guys are here for our benefit."

"The hell they are." He squinted his eyes at Skuz and lowered his voice. "You'd better keep him safe, or I'm going hunting. You get me?"

"I get the not so subtle threat, yes," Skuz said.

"I don't do subtle."

"That's why mom left us, Dad." Irving slapped his dad on the back as he limped past. "I'm ready, guys."

"You may want to spend the night at a motel, sir," Skuz said. "For your own safety."

"Shut the hell up, purple boy." He slammed the door in his face.

"Your dad's kind of a dick, dude." Skuz turned away from the door and threw his arm around Irving's shoulders. "Still, you have to respect him. Most dads wouldn't point guns at two guys in gang colors."

"I'm not sure if that's smart though. He's always been a little belligerent."

"We've got a plan, buddy." Garret slid open the side of the van and helped Irving inside. "We'll tell you on the way." He climbed in behind him, while Skuz circled around the back and climbed in.

"What's the plan, boys?" Irving buckled his seat belt.

"We're going to take them out in one swoop. Sound good?" Skuz asked. "It'll be a little risky, but what do you say?"

"If it'll work, sure."

"Tony," Richard looked up into the rearview mirror, "make the call, and be convincing. No is not an option for this guy."

"Got it, Pres." Tony pulled out his cell and dialed. "Yo, Larry? It's me, Tony. We need a big favor from you. What? Are you really going to say that when I can tell your wife everything about your two's meeting. She might not be so happy with you, you know. It'd be a right shame if she divorced you and took the kid away without so much as visitation."

"God damn," Irving whispered. "He's going right for the jugular."

"Watch the master at work," Garret whispered back.

"Damn it, man. All we need is a little package from your

work. You don't have to take it anywhere. Just have your break room window open at a specified time and make a hand off. That's all. Just make damned sure the stuff is slow acting and contained. Yeah, powder would work best. That would spread if they opened it, right? Alright, have it ready by..." he trailed off. "Hold on." He placed a palm over the receiver of the phone. "When?"

"Have it ready by noon," Richard said.

"Noon. Someone will be there to pick it up. If you talk to anyone about this, and that includes when people come asking, your life falls apart. You understand me? Good. Now what side of the building is this room on and what floor?" He paused. "Third floor, west side, and furthest to the right. Got it. Have a nice sleep." He hung up. "It's set up." He snapped the phone, rolled down the nearest window, and tossed it.

"Okay then. Now we rely on the Outback boys to find where we're delivering our little care package," Richard smirked. "You always know how to convince someone, Tony. What do you have on the guy anyway?"

"That story? Originally his wife was going on a blind date with some jackass. He was originally her stalker of sorts. He told me what was going on, and I made sure the guy didn't show up. He did."

"That's creepy," Ann muttered. "You helped him get away with that?"

"Apparently she liked him enough to get married. But she has a quick temper and flies off the handle readily."

"Sounds like they're made for each other. One's conniving, the other fickle."

"Pretty much," Richard said. "Now take us to Garret's, prospect. We need to set up rotating shifts tonight. It'll be the last time boys, so suffer through it."

"I'll take first shift," Garret said. "Our building's big, so having at least three at a time would be better. One on each exposed side of the building would be better than wandering back and forth. It'd be a lot harder to miss someone trying to sneak in if we're watching every entrance."

"Skuz," Richard said, "you and I will accompany Garret. We'll let Ann here get some sleep."

"I knew you always liked me." Ann leaned forward and giggled.

"Don't go having daydreams now." Richard looked to his side at the passing cityscape. "I just need to talk to Garret about tomorrow, that's all."

"Sure it is." Ann rolled her eyes. She shifted her gaze to Garret at her side. "I need to talk to you later. Wake me up when you get inside. It'll probably be my turn to take watch then."

"I'll go in the next wave," Irving said.

"No, man, you're healing," Garret said. "I'll take a double shift. You need to rest."

"I can handle it."

"I'm sure you can, but I don't want your dad shooting me in the face either."

"Yeah," Skuz said. "That dude is intimidating."

"At least let me watch the lobby."

"Fair enough," Richard said.

Back at Garret's Apartment...

"You watch the entrance while me and Garret talk," Richard said to Irving in the nearby chair. "I'll come get you when we're done, and then you can feel free to doze off."

"I've been waiting to be useful again. Take your time, fellas." Irving turned the seat to face the entrance. His hand fell to his hip and rested against the firearm in its holster. "I got this."

"You heard the man." Richard turned and led the now trio outside. "Skuz, secure the southern side. Garret, come with me." He led Garret to the west side. "Stay on this side." He turned the corner. "There." He twisted his neck and kept watch as he talked. "It'll finally be done by tomorrow. Be ready to start making collecting runs the day after tomorrow. We need all the money we can get to pay off the smurfs, if we want to make all that meth."

"That's a bit like putting the cart before the horse, isn't it? We need to focus on tomorrow's pickup and delivery. We'll need to disguise the package with, at the bare minimum, the postage and a return address. Otherwise they might not even open the thing."

"That means we'll also have to have the delivery man sit near the house until the mail runs. Otherwise it'd be suspicious."

"Which means we'll have to hurry. Whoever's picking up the virus will have to hurry back and hand me the box. Make sure they're in plain clothes and in a non-descript vehicle. I don't need them drawing attention at the handoff."

"Obviously," Richard said. "Then once that's done, no one can resist opening a package addressed to them. Right?"

"It's always been a weakness of mine. I assume it's the same for them. Then a few of them will run home to their boss. You really think they'll be dumb enough?"

"They're not bio-molecular scientists," Richard said.

"They won't think they're infected with a deadly contagion. They'll just know they need to report this new development. That's the flaw of dictatorships. Someone always needs to run home to the boss to report and get new orders. That's what we're taking advantage of here."

"Yeah. They maybe don't even know how to read, if the rumors are true." Garret kept watch and pulled out a cigarette. He lit it and exhaled a cloud of smoke. "You really think they kidnap kids from school down there in Mexico and train them to become hitmen?"

"Judging by the level of intellect from their peons so far, I'd say so. The only one to even scratch us worth a damn was that sniper that winged Irving. Skuz got a scratch from their rank and file."

"It was too bad that guy shot himself before the police apprehended him. I was hoping to meet him while I was in lockup before."

"It's probably better you didn't. You'd never have gotten out if you'd shanked anyone else. You're lucky to have gotten away with just shanking that smelly bomb maker."

Garret took a deep drag, causing the end of the cancer stick to glow bright orange. "Word around the place was that his lawyer was coming in frequently. I had to make that happen or we'd all be in there."

"We need a backup plan in case this guy at the DDC gets the same idea as your mad bomber. Any ideas?"

"Besides Tony threatening to ruin his family life? You really think we need another?"

"Eh," Richard spat on the black top, "a man can get brave if his family life sucks. He may do something he regrets later to piss off a nagging wife for example. I'd prefer a little more leverage just in case. You can never have too much. Remember that."

"Well," Garret threw the cigarette down and snuffed it out with his boots, "we could always send Irving out to take a photo of the guy's kids going to school. That'd freak him out. He may gamble with his wife, but you think he'll gamble with his kids' lives?"

"No. No, he would not. Good idea. That way, everything in his life crumbles if he feels talkative. Remember, we don't hurt kids, but he doesn't need to know that. As far as he's concerned we're monsters, and that's how it has to be."

"Obviously. If that fails, we can consider force as a last resort. Though I've no idea if that'd cause more problems than it'd solve with him working for the DDC."

"Those egghead types always have tons of people missing them. They'd start investigations if they caught so much as a whiff of foul play. Let's try not to find out. We've got everything set up. Let's just focus on executing."

"Who's going to make the pickup? Tony, I assume, since he knows the guy? That means I'm driving."

"It'd be for the best. He knows Tony. We do not want that little twig boy panicking up there. While you two are doing that, the rest of us will be at the Outback Boys' place. When you're done, give us a call. We'll meet up at the address they give us. Then it's just a little delivery, and we're out of this war. All we'll have to do then is play defense, while their ranks are torn apart due to deadly contagion." Richard chuckled. "It's genius."

"I don't know about you, but I'm going to be wearing one of those face masks until right before I step out of the van."

"You're paranoid. That guy is going to package it up nice and tight. He doesn't want a major public emergency. I get where you're coming from though. Buy enough for everyone when you get some. It's better to be safe than sorry when it comes to deadly viruses, or whatever it will be."

"We'll also need to find a new place."

"Yeah, I always keep a few places lined up just in case this happens."

"You kept a list of locales just in case something happened to ours?"

"Didn't you read comics as a kid? My favorite character always had an answer to everything that could conceivably go wrong. I've set aside some money over the past twenty years, so we'll be fine if we can supplement that with our meth money."

Garret laughed. "I never imagined you were the type to read comics as a kid."

"Of course. It was that or study."

"So we have the money and the next place lined up. The only thing we need concern ourselves with after this is the current money stream. Provided this goes off, we're looking at easy street."

"Don't get cocky now. That's always when things go south."

"Yeah." Garret looked down the barren night street. The sounds of distant horns and screams echoed in his ears. "Don't I know it."

The door to Garret's right opened, and Ann came outside. "I couldn't sleep." She rubbed her eyes. "Where is everyone?"

"Rich is around this corner, and Skuz is on the other side of the building."

"Smart." She turned the corner. "You can head inside. I've got this shift."

"I'm not going to argue." Richard passed Ann and Garret. He pulled open the lobby doors and looked over to Garret. "You two have fun, but not too much fun." He disappeared inside, and the glass door slammed shut.

"What's up?"

"Have you all considered what might happen if something goes wrong tomorrow?"

"What's this about all of a sudden?"

Ann shifted at his side. She looked away from Garret toward the other side of the building. "I don't like this."

"You don't like what?"

"Playing God with a disease like this."

"It's not my top idea either, but Rich knows what he's doing."

"Does he?" Ann asked. "Do you know what could happen if that stuff gets out of containment? Do you have any idea? Thousands could die. I'm talking all of us and most of the town."

"You're nervous. I get it." Garret crossed his arms. "I don't relish the idea of lugging around death in a box either you know."

"I just don't want to be responsible for the death of kids in this town. I may not value scum's lives, but innocents? This is getting too risky."

"What are you here to say? You know I can't stop this. It's already in motion. What do you want me to do?"

"I don't know." Ann kicked a nearby pebble into the road. "I don't know if I can be part of this."

"I understand that. All I'd ask is that you keep it to yourself. You're not part of this club, so that's your choice."

"I'll never rat. I'm covered in just as much dirt as your club is. It'd be suicide."

"Then we don't have a problem. Just get a good night's sleep. Sleep in past noon, and this will all be done before you wake up."

"That's certainly one option."

Garret turned the corner and stepped forward. He

wrapped his arms around her shoulders. "I knew you were the bigger softie."

"Normally I'd punch the hell out of you for saying that."

"Not this time?"

"No."

"I knew I was a lucky man."

"Don't go counting your chickens yet, sport."

"Hm?"

"Nothing." Ann broke free from the embrace and backed up. "Nothing at all."

"You're acting a little odd."

"Just promise me you'll treat that box like a newborn baby. Don't so much as drop it roughly, or the consequences could be all our deaths. It could even turn into a national incident. Which, even if we survived it, we'd be in shit."

"I'll treat it as if it was my own kid, my own deathly infected baby that I'm about to leave on a random stranger's porch."

She delivered a straight punch into his right shoulder causing him to stumble back. "Be serious, jackass. This is not a joking matter. Have you even thought that this could trigger a global infection scenario?"

"I think you've read too many dystopian novels."

"Contagion rarely stays isolated. Before anyone shows symptoms, they get on planes to other countries."

"I'm pretty sure we're not going to end the world with this."

"Pretty sure? That's it? You're willing to bet on that?"

"I gamble with my life every day."

Ann's face soured. "So, you're betting with everyone's now? Because that's what it sounds like. All those innocent babies around here will be bet too you know. Why don't you think about that out here all night?" She stomped off and slammed the door, leaving Garret behind in silence.

"Fuck." He went back to his post and leaned his head back against the brick. He gazed up into the endless sparkly abyss above. "The worst part is I know she's right. God, I hate when that happens."

"I heard that all the way on the other side of the building." Skuz appeared from the other side of the building. He kept watch on his side and beckoned Garret over.

Garret approached his best friend and leaned against the building around the corner. "How much did you hear of that?"

"Pretty much just after she mentioned the babies around here." Skuz's voice grew softer. "She's not entirely wrong on this one. I once watched a documentary that showed how easily communicable diseases are spread."

"Whose side are you on?"

"Yours, but I'm not going to lie to you either. That's the deal we've had since we were teenagers."

"The odds of that happening are tiny." Garret jammed his hands inside his pockets. "It'll just be some gangsters is all."

"I suspect it's the same for you and Rich, but I would have never voted for this plan if we'd had any other choice. These guys proved they can stay ahead of us and have superior firepower when they sent that chopper after us."

"At least I brought those countermeasures back to the apartment for when we go tomorrow."

"I fail to see how emp grenades are going to help us deliver a package, but it's better safe than sorry I suppose. Still," Skuz sniffed, "let's just hope they go straight to their boss. If they start wandering around, this could turn out bad."

"We do what we must." Garret hung his head.

"We tell ourselves that to assuage our conscience," Skuz paused, "but the truth is, we're worried. We just won't admit it."

"Being worried doesn't help a thing. All worry does is cause panic and cause your hands to shake, neither of which will help our predicament."

"It still wouldn't hurt to bring an airtight box when we pick up the package. Why take chances, right?"

"You're right. I think I have a big enough airtight crate we can shove in the back of the van tomorrow morning."

"Hey, Garret?" Skuz asked.

"Yeah?"

"This will really be the last of this shit, right?"

"Yeah, buddy. I'm going to make sure of it."

"Good. Because I'm tired of this shit. I just want to go back to before. You remember before this beef? We'd just go around collecting and making bank without the slightest care. No one messed with us."

"Cartel's do tend to expand territory when given the chance. It was inevitable that they'd try to come north of the border. We're just denying them entry is all. Hell, the police should be thanking us when you think about it. How many of those murderers have we put down so far in this war? Probably half of them had given those infamous oil baths in the desert."

"Oil baths?

"You know the ones. Where they knock someone out and stuff them in a barrel full of oil. They wake them up and then light it up with them wide awake and conscious."

"Holy hell. They really are animals."

"That's one of the reasons I don't feel bad doing this. They deserve it. They shot Irv, they tried to kill us all, and they will not stop unless we force the issue. We don't have a choice here, don't forget that. If they knew where your family's place was, they'd lock them inside and burn them alive. Never forget that. We're just striking first."

"I suppose so."

"I know so."

"We did the same thing though."

"What?" Garret turned the corner. "What did you say?"

Skuz looked over at Garret. "I said we burned their family alive. Shot them too. Don't you remember?"

"War is hell. The more brutal it is, the shorter it lasts."

"Where did you get that from?"

"Some military general in the past. The point is, we must do everything to end it so that it ends sooner."

"I'm just saying, they're not going to quit until they're all dead, and that's our fault. I get what you're saying, and you're probably right. I just don't have to like what we're going to do."

"All I ask is that you have my back through this." Garret extended his hand.

Skuz looked down at the hand and swatted it away. He looked up at Garret's confused face and grabbed the hand before pulling him into a brief hug. "You already know that answer. Don't ask dumb questions, you idiot. When I said I'd be with you through hell and back, I meant it. We may go to hell over this, but I'm not abandoning you at the gates. If I'm going in, we're going to kick some ass together."

"You always had a flair for the dramatic and melodramatic. I mean, just look at that hair."

"You and everyone else is just jealous." Skuz brushed the purple hair on top of his scalp and then grazed over the shaved sides of his head. "This is all the rage nowadays."

"You look like a blooming moron. Go all or nothing, not

half and half."

"You're just an old fuddy duddy. That's all that is."

Garret let loose a hearty laugh. "If you say so."

"Better than that honey blonde hair mess you've got going on there." Skuz poked Garret's forehead. "You look like a wannabe movie star with that crap."

"If we're going to hell, I may as well look respectable." Garret reached up and rubbed his bare chin.

"I guess so." Skuz returned to his original position around the corner. "Besides, I'm more worried about the aftermath. The pickup won't be too hard. That's assuming the guy doesn't panic. I don't envy Tony. It won't be easy to remain subtle when you're climbing the fire escape of the local DDC branch. Hell, it might be illegal."

"You think it's illegal to use a fire escape?"

"When you don't even work there? Quite possibly. I'd imagine so."

"He'll be low key. If we're lucky, some peeping tom will just think he's there to see his girlfriend. I think you're paranoid though."

"Paranoid or not, I'm just thinking of all the angles like you taught me."

"I can't fault that. You're finally listening. Now if only we could get you to do that with women, you'd be set."

The two shared a laugh and stopped when they heard a distant voice speaking Spanish. "Did you hear that?" Skuz asked in a soft voice. "It sounds like it came from this way." He pointed over the nearby fence.

"Fine, let's check it out." Garret pulled out his .357 magnum and Skuz his semi-automatic handgun. He took the lead and peeked around the corner of the nearby concrete barrier. "It's some hood rats, you paranoid lout. Still, they're coming this way. Stay ready. They look like they're looking for trouble. I don't see any weapons except a bad attitude, but they could be concealing them. Stay on your toes."

"If they're looking for it, why don't we oblige them?" Skuz asked. "You know, show them how this life will look down the line?"

"You mean scare them straight? Sounds like it could be fun and save us rivals down the line. I'm in." He tucked his six shooter into his belt.

Garret and Skuz stepped out onto the street, directly in the path of the group of young men.

"Get out of our way, old man," the one in front said.

"Is that how kids treat their elders now?" Skuz asked Garret.

"What the hell are you kids doing out this late in this part of town?" Garret asked. He raised his shirt, revealing his magnum in his belt line. "You might run into the wrong sort around here."

"I ain't afraid of that thing. You're not going to shoot me."

"Is that right?" Garret pulled out the weapon and flicked open the chamber. "Got all the bullets in there." He pulled back the hammer. "You sure about that?"

'Pablo," one of the smaller boys tugged on the leader's sleeve, "maybe we should just go."

"Yeah, listen to the smart one there," Skuz said.

Pablo wiped away beads of sweat dripping down his face. "Fine, we were just going out for some beer anyway. We don't need this right now." He led the group of young boys back the way they had come.

"Did we just do a public service?" Garret asked.

"I think so. Their mothers probably would want to thank us, if you know what I mean."

"You always were into MILFS."

14

Garret rolled over in his bed and rubbed his eyes. "Babe?" He looked at the empty spot on the bed next to him and saw from the red glowing numbers that it was now almost six a.m. "She must have gotten up early." He swung his legs over the side of the bed, stumbled to his feet, and went over to the closet. He opened the doors and pulled on a black shirt. He walked over to the nearby chair and put on his kutte, then walked outside his bedroom. "Time to wake up, boys." He flipped the nearby light switch and illuminated the large living room. He stepped over a few sleeping bags and made his way to the kitchen. He was making coffee when an annoyed voice interrupted him.

"Is it already that time?" Richard asked while sitting up. "It seems like I just went to bed."

"It sure is." Garret placed the pot onto the coffee machine. "You haven't seen Ann, have you?"

"Last I saw, she was going outside for her turn on watch."

"Yeah, me too. She should have been back inside by now though. I'll head out there and tell her to come back inside. You all just focus on waking up and getting ready for today."

"Will do." Richard rubbed his eyes and looked to his side toward Lucien's snoring form. He crawled out of his sleeping bag and kicked Lucien's back. "Wake up."

"I'll leave you to it." Garret grabbed his coat from the hanger near the front door, put it on, and headed outside. He reached the bottom floor and saw Irving sleeping in the chair he'd left him in. He poked his shoulder causing him to wake with a jump. "Easy there. It's time to get up, dude."

"Oh, sorry. I must have dozed off."

"I don't blame you. It must have been boring down here by yourself. My bad for not bringing you back up."

"I can get back myself." He stood up with wobbly legs. "I'm already regaining strength. You don't have to worry about me."

"Don't push yourself now. Are you sure?"

"Dude, go." Irving took a few unsteady steps toward the nearby elevator and pressed the button. "I've got this."

"By the way, have you seen Ann recently?"

"I saw her stomp outside. She seemed pissed for some reason. Was that your doing?"

"Something like that."

"Then tread with caution, brother. Do you have a plan for how you're going to diffuse that?"

"You're going to give me love advice now?"

"If you want it."

"I'm good."

"Alright then." The bell above dinged and the doors in front of Irving slid open. He hobbled inside and pressed a button. "Be careful, and don't let her get the better of you."

"You know it." Garret watched the doors close and turned his attention back to the exit. "Now if only I knew how I was going to fix it." He pushed the double glass doors and headed outside. He looked to his left and saw Tony shivering in the cold.

"Is it that time finally?" he asked.

"Yeah, head inside and warm yourself, man. Is Ann out here?"

"She came out earlier. She headed around the back." He walked by and stopped shoulder to shoulder with Garret. "Be careful, bro. She seemed like a walking hornet's nest. I don't know what you did, but she was in no mood to talk."

"I've been hearing that a lot."

"You want me to come along?"

"Nah, dude. Get inside and warm up. We don't need people getting sick."

"Good luck." Tony headed inside the glass doors.

He wandered around the nearby side of the building, only to see Harold keeping watch.

"Hey, big guy. Head inside and get yourself some coffee. I've got this."

"Oh, Mr. Price."

"Call me Garret."

"Okay."

"Is Ann over there?" He pointed toward the corner near Harold.

"What? She told me you sent her to gather provisions for today."

"She what?"

"She left like an hour ago. I thought you told her to."

"Shit." Garret's breath was visible in the cold. "No, I never sent her out."

"I'm sorry, sir. She was very convincing."

"I bet she was. Did she say when she was coming back?"

"It should be soon. She said she was going to the sports

store a couple blocks away. I was trying to keep watch on both sides of the building until she came back."

Garret rubbed his temples. "Damn that woman. What is she doing?"

"Sir?

"Just get inside out of this cold. We'll deal with this complication later."

"You don't have to tell me twice." Harold walked back along with Garret. "She seemed distressed."

"I bet she did."

"You'll find another girl, Garret."

"I appreciate the vote of confidence, kid, but for once I actually don't want another woman."

Harold opened the double doors and let Garret take the lead. "You mean you're in -"

"That's all I'm saying to a prospect. I'll tell you the rest after you're a full-fledged member."

"She'll come back."

Garret pushed the elevator button and turned to look at Harold. "No, she won't; but I appreciate what you're trying to do." He stepped inside the elevator.

"I guess we should focus on the job today then."

"That's the spirit. Keep your head clear and focused."

The doors opened revealing the long corridor ahead. Garret led the pair back to the apartment. He inserted the key into the lock and headed inside. He held the door open for Harold behind him. "Is everyone awake now?"

"Close enough." Lucien upended his mug of coffee.

"Where's your girl?" Richard asked from the dining table beside the old man.

"She took off somewhere. She lied to the prospect and told him I'd ordered her to go out for supplies."

"You think she'll come back?"

"No."

"Will she be a problem?"

"I don't think so," Garret said.

"Then let's get ready for today, and be prepared for the worst-case scenario. Because of this complication, we'll have to adjust in case it does happen. Garret, I want you to try and call her. Figure out what she's doing if she'll pick up. If she's gone, that's fine. We can't afford having her mucking this up."

"I was going to anyway. Give me a minute." He walked back to his bedroom, pushed open the door, and picked up the cell sitting on the nightstand near his bed. He flipped it open and dialed as he sat on the bed. "Come on. At least pick up and have the decency to tell me why you left." He hung his head as the fifth ring echoed in his ear, then heard a click and a voice.

"I'm not coming back," was the first thing she said.

"That's your business. You have any plans on interfering in mine today?"

"I'm on my way out of the state in case your 'business' gets screwed up. You don't have to worry about me. I'm meeting up with Katie. Don't tell Irving. He'd just end up like you. Being desperate is not a good look."

"Don't flatter yourself."

"Always quick with the one-liners. Let's hope your next girl appreciates it."

"We'll see." Garret hung up without further ado. "Bitch." He pocketed the phone and made his way back to the living room. "She won't be a problem. She's high tailing it in case we lose containment on our package."

"I wouldn't have taken her for a coward." Richard shook his head. "No matter. This changes nothing as long as she won't say anything."

"Where do you want me today? Am I going with you all or hanging back here again?" Irving asked from the sofa near the wall.

"We're going to be short on space in the back as it is," Garret said. "Staying here would be best. We don't want that box getting jostled around because there's too many of us in the van. That's a recipe for disaster."

"Got it." Irving grabbed the remote control for the nearby television, flipped it on, and lowered the volume. "I'll watch the place while you're gone. The prospect and I can hold it down."

"While you're doing that, Garret, Skuz, and Tony will go to the meeting spot and pick up our package. Lucien and I will go ahead toward the Outback Boys' headquarters. We'll meet there and head out together. We'll find out where they are and then be on our way. Make sure to bring the emp grenades."

"It's a good thing I brought them back from the clubhouse before those animals burned it down." Garret jogged back to his room and opened the dresser. He opened the false wall in the back and leaned inside. He picked up the box and lugged it back to the main room. He placed them down on the kitchen table. "Everybody take one. You never know when you might need it. Just remember they will knock out car engines, lights, anything you need." He shoved one of the devices into his pocket and started handing the rest out.

"Just remember to not screw yourselves in the process," Richard said. "It'll stop anything electronic, including anything around you. It's a double-edged sword we have here."

"Meaning no pulling the pin in the van because you were messing around." Garret glared momentarily at Skuz.

"Anyway, my group is going to head out now. We need to find a good place to watch from until the appointed time. Tony, Skuz, you're with me. Irv, you watch my place. If anything happens, go get a weapon from my cabinet." He tossed the last emp grenade to him. "Please try not to use this, but if you have to, I understand."

"You just don't want your television fried."

"I'd rather have it fried than Irv here shot full of holes." He looked back to Irving. "If you have to get out in a hurry," he walked over to the nearby window and opened it, revealing a fire escape down to the alley below, "use this. It'll suck on that leg, but it's better than the alternative. If I were you, I'd throw that under their vehicle during your getaway."

"I'll be fine." Irving stretched out and placed his hands behind his head.

"Don't take it too easy until we get back," Tony said.

"Alright, boys." Richard clapped his hands. "Let's get going."

Hours later outside the DDC...

"The window just opened." Garret lowered the binoculars and handed them to Tony beside him in the passenger's seat. "It looks like he's playing ball."

"That must mean he's done packaging the stuff," Skuz said. "There's no way he'd open that if it was still airborne."

"Which means it's my turn now, gentlemen." Tony placed the binoculars down on the arm rest between seats. "Wish me luck."

"Just be careful climbing down with that thing," Skuz

said. "Tuck it under one arm as you climb down or something."

"That was the initial plan."

"I'll go with you." Garret raised a hand and silenced Tony. "I won't go up there and spook him. I just don't want you getting caught with your pants down when you're holding something that could kill us and the general public. You're going to be dangling defenseless as you climb down." He turned and looked back at Skuz in the back seat. "You take the driver's seat and keep the engine running. We may need to get out of here in a heartbeat."

"You always get the fun jobs."

"You call sitting near dumpsters while you get the air conditioning fun?" Garret chuckled. "Let's go." He and Tony flung the doors open and stepped out onto the pavement. They walked shoulder to shoulder toward the building's alley.

"Did you ever imagine doing something like this when we joined the club?" Tony asked.

"Can't say that I did. I thought the worst I'd experience was a fire fight or something. This?" He shook his head. "I guess desperate times call for desperate measures."

Tony grabbed the ladder leading up and rested a foot on the bottom rung. "Brother, this is our best shot, and we all know it. Be back in a minute." He climbed up until he'd reached the third floor. He ducked down and shimmied his way toward the open window. He poked his head up and saw a lone man tapping his foot as he was staring at the window.

"Finally." He picked up the nearby box with great care and carried it over to the open window. He set the bottom of the package on the windowsill. He held the package steady with one hand and pushed up his glasses with the other. "Now be careful with this. If this gets out to the general public there will be a huge investigation and untold amounts of death. In accordance to your wishes, there's only the one airtight layer so that when it opens, whoever's there is infected. I don't want to know who. I don't care. We're done after this. I owe you nothing. Just don't get any innocents infected is all I ask. That would make it an impossibility for me to remain under the radar. They'd start investigations until they found out how the stuff got out, and they wouldn't stop until they got an answer."

"I get it. Just keep quiet about this, and it will all go away." Tony picked up the plain brown box and tucked it under his left arm. "Nothing will happen to any innocents. We don't want that heat either. Now shut this window and act normal the rest of the day. You're done." Tony turned away from the window and began the decent down to the alley toward Garret. "Heads up." He dropped down beside him. "Got it. Now let's get out of here. I feel uneasy just being near this thing. I'd rather get this done as soon as possible."

"I get that." Garret snuck a glance at the box. "It looks innocent enough, but it has the power to kill everyone in the city. You're right. I feel nervous just being near the thing. That guy may have been a wuss, but he was the one to package this, right? You've got to give him credit for that."

"True."

Garret opened the back and gingerly loaded the box in. "You keep this still. I don't want this sliding around and bumping into anything."

Tony got in and grasped the package. "You and me both."

Garret climbed into the front and flipped open his

phone as the van moved forward. "I'll tell Rich we're on our way."

"I can't believe we're really doing this." Tony's arm encircled the box to keep it steady as the van took a sharp right turn.

"Yeah, we got it," Garret said into the phone. "We're on our way there now. You almost there?"

"We're a few minutes out," Richard said. "We'll wait there for you three to arrive and then we'll make our move. We've got the labels here. We'll make it really attractive so anyone will want to open it. We just need the address to complete it."

"You're sure they'll have the place we need?"

"I called Eric earlier. He said they'd found the place, but didn't want to reveal it over the phone. By the time you get here, all we'll have to do is slap them on."

"Sounds good. We'll be there in a little bit. Stay sharp over there."

"You too."

Garret hung up and looked over to Skuz in the driver's seat. "Let's get over there."

Meanwhile back at Garret's apartment...

Irving laid on the sofa and rested his head on the end. He yawned and was interrupted by his cell phone ringing. "Who the hell would call right now?" He answered, bringing the phone up to his ear. "Yeah?"

A familiar feminine voice rang in his ears. "Open the door."

"What?"

"Open the damned door, you idiot," the voice insisted, louder this time. "There's no time to argue."

"Katie?" He pushed himself up to a sitting position, then hopped to a standing position. "How would you even know where I am?"

"Annie told me what's going on."

Irving hobbled to the door and peeked out of the peep hole. Sure enough, Katie stood in the hallway. He unlocked the door and threw it open. "I never thought I'd see you again."

She pushed past him. "I wasn't planning on it until I heard this retarded plan your boss came up with. I'm getting you out of this. Now start packing. Quick!"

"I can't just leave like this. I need to tell the prospect. He's sleeping right now."

"You don't have a choice. Trust me on this. You're leaving with me. The prospect will be fine."

"Why are you so adamant?"

She stopped in her tracks and turned back to him. She stomped over, grasped his shoulders, and lowered her voice. "I can't tell you that right now, but, for your own safety, trust me. You used to trust me."

Irving's eyes softened and looked away. "Alright. I'll go, but I should be back by tonight. The guys will be back."

Katie turned her back. "That's fine."

"I don't have anything here, so let's go now." He placed a hand on her shoulder causing her to turn back to him. He flashed her a warm smile. "I'm just a little slow after our last meeting." He limped toward the door and turned back to her. "What's wrong? A group of the cartel on their way here?"

"Yeah. That's it. We saw them loading for bear and

heading this way." She hurried over, grabbed his hand, and dragged him out of the door.

He kicked the door closed behind him. "I thought you left the city and I'd never see you again." He followed behind her down the long hallway toward the elevators.

"No, I simply got an apartment here. I've been in constant contact with Ann this whole time. She's kept me informed." She jammed a finger onto the down arrow. "I was waiting for you to get out." She looked down at the carpet. "It turns out, this is the best I could hope for. I was hoping you'd have common sense and quit after nearly dying. It turns out you're dumber than I was hoping."

"Well that's a little har-" He was interrupted by her abruptly turning to him, grabbing his shoulders, pulling him close, and planting a kiss on his lips. She got down from her tip toes and licked her lips.

"Was that too harsh?" The elevator dinged as the doors nearby opened. "I'll have to work on that." She led the way into the elevator and dragged him inside before pressing the ground floor button. "Just trust me. This is the best for you." The doors opened, revealing Ann in the apartment lobby watching the front doors.

She glanced over her shoulders. "Alright, we need to hurry. They'll be here soon." She jogged over and took the other side of Irving. The three left the lobby in a hurry toward Ann's nearby car.

"I can't believe they found us." Irving ducked into the car and scooted over. "They must have followed us. Why didn't they hit us last night?"

"Who knows?" Ann plopped into the driver's seat and twisted the key in the ignition. "All we need to worry about is getting out of here."

Katie took the seat next to Irving and slammed the door shut. "We're good."

The car's engine roared to life as the vehicle pulled out onto the empty road. She pulled onto a nearby freeway. Ann dug into her pocket and handed a phone back to Katie. "Make the call."

"Calling the boys to warn them?"

"Something like that." Katie rubbed Irving's knee as she dialed with her other hand. Once the ringing stopped, her hand reached into her own pants pocket. "The Order is making their move. Be on the lookout for a white van."

"What the fuck? Who are you -" Irving attempted to gain control over the phone as Katie's hand flew out of her pocket with a thin piece of wet material clutched tightly. She climbed on top of him and covered Irving's nose. His muffled noises turned to incoherent rambling after a few minutes and later faded into eventual silence. She climbed off him and guided his head to her shoulder.

"Never mind that noise. I'm telling you that they've stolen a contagion from the DDC. They're going to try and unleash it on their rivals, ES-15. I don't know where they are, but you need to take this seriously. I don't know. Do your job and stake out all their known locations or something. When you do, go in strapped. They won't go down without a fight. How do I know? One of their members felt guilty and felt like coming clean. He wants to make a deal for immunity." She looked over toward Irving's unconscious form. She ran the back of her hand over his cheek and a fleeting smile crossed her face. "We'll be in touch." She hung up and filed the phone away in a hurry.

"He's going to hate you when he wakes up."

"It's for his own good."

"Let's hope he sees it that way."

"I will convince him one way or the other." She cupped his face in her palm and rubbed his chin. "It was the only way. Besides, I'd be more worried if I were you. Garret wasn't exactly tolerant of betrayal himself, and he's the Sergeant-at-Arms. He'll be coming for blood. It's his job."

"With any luck we won't have to deal with them. The cops will. If push comes to shove, I'll handle him."

"I don't know what you ever saw in him anyway."

Ann sighed as she stopped at a red light. "You've never had infatuation with a bad boy you thought you could reform? Really? Who's that beside you again?"

"Fair point, but I didn't revel in their little boys club for months before quitting."

"I thought I wanted back in. I couldn't be party to this. Even I have my breaking point. Your boyfriend there was one of only two who voted nay to their little plan."

"Of course he wouldn't vote for it." Katie looked to her left at Irving's unconscious swaying body. His head eventually fell and landed on her lap. She placed a palm down and began rubbing the back of his head. "He's not like the others."

"We'll see."

15

The van drove into the Outback Boys' parking lot and pulled up next to their building. Everyone filed out.

"There they are," a loud voice said from the front door of the main building. Eric appeared and beckoned them inside. "Get in here. We have a lot to talk about today."

"You heard the man." Richard led the group into the base. They entered a dim room kept illuminated by a few hanging lights placed strategically throughout the room. They came to a large circular table where they all took a seat.

"Right, here's the skinny." Eric was the last to take a seat, next to Richard. "We have the location of one of their places. It's not where their leader is, but we know for a fact that cartel members stay there."

"That's more than enough," Richard said.

"Yeah," Garret said. "We're not asking for miracles here."

"It's none of my business, and feel free to say as much, but what exactly are you lads going for here?" Eric asked.

"I'd love to tell you, but you know how this works," Richard said. "The more people that know, the more risk.

That's just the nature of this business. Just trust me when I say, we're going to end this war today. Period. Full fucking stop."

"I'd love to know how you're going to pull that off, but fair enough." Eric dug around in his coat pocket and placed a folded paper on the table between him and Richard. "Here's the address. There shouldn't be too many people there according to Kelly. He scouted it out himself."

"That will work," Lucien said. "We don't need anything fancy for this plan."

"You're not going to end up on the six o'clock news for this, right?" Eric asked. "We can't be associated with that."

"No, of course not. We're professionals. Press is bad for business," Richard said.

"Alright then. I'll send Kelly with you if you'd like. He's my best man, and he knows the area better than anyone else here. With him, whatever you'll be doing has a better shot at success."

Garret glanced at Richard. "I'm not sure that's a good idea."

"We appreciate the offer. We're keeping this one in house. We'll compensate you next month for this."

The front door opened again with Kelly's voice accompanying it. "Oy, they're here?" He strode up to the table. "I assume you all want me to go?"

"They're saying no," Eric said.

"That's bollocks. But fine, as long as we're paid."

"We appreciate you finding this information and all the work that went into it," Garret said. "We know this wasn't easy. We're just set on doing the actual hands-on work ourselves. You know, to save you boys the trouble."

"That's awfully kind of you," Eric said. "Don't let us stop you. Do what you mean to do. Of course you realize if this goes sideways, we don't know you, and you don't know us."

"You don't have to tell us twice."

Lucien snorted. "Same goes for you, Eric. We don't want rumors floating around the street that we're doing anything."

"Of course."

Kelly leaned on the back of Garret's seat. "We know how to keep our mouths shut. It's hard not to when I'm stuck here for the rest of the day anyway."

"Why don't you go ahead and attend to the rest of your duties?" Eric glanced over at Kelly. "We'll finish up here and be outside in a few minutes."

"No skin off my nose." Kelly pushed off the chair and sidled out the same door he came in and waited beside it. "I'll be waiting outside then."

"Forgive him. He's just enthusiastic with his job."

"That's better than the alternative," Richard said. "We appreciate the zealous way he got us our location. You hear that, Kelly? We love your work."

"Always nice to be appreciated, boys." Kelly exited the building and closed the door behind him.

"Anyway," Eric said, "I sure hope you're right about this plan of yours. We're starting to see more resistance on the streets because of our alliance. If this keeps up, I'm not sure how we'll adjust. Drive-bys are just the least of our dealer's problems. They're stepping up their game. They're sending hitmen to our best earners' homes. This is quickly getting out of control. You're sure this will end this war? Because it's starting to become untenable."

"Believe me. I know all about that," Richard said. He slammed his fist onto the wooden table. "This plan will put an end to their local charter. That I can guarantee you, so long as that intel is good."

"You have my word. So, don't let me keep you." Eric pushed his chair out with a screech along the floor. "I have to go put out the last of these fires before you permanently extinguish them. You know, just to be safe. Good luck in your venture."

"We appreciate it." Richard got up and walked over to Eric. The two wrapped their arms around each other for a moment and slapped each other's backs before taking a step back. "I got this, old friend."

"Good."

"We're moving out," Richard said after he backed up from the embrace. "No sense keeping our allies waiting."

"I hear that," Lucien said with a grunt as he got up.

"You all got a printer here?" Garret asked.

"Sure." Eric pointed toward the corner of the room. "Why?"

"Do you mind if we use that for a minute?"

"I'm intrigued. Sure."

"Thanks." Garret swiped up the folded paper from the tabletop and headed over to the personal computer. A few moments later the printer roared to life and printed out. He took the paper and came back. "It's a good thing I had Irving teach me that before we left." He held up the paper. "I've got the last piece right here."

"Then we're good." Skuz jumped up.

"We're going to go fix both our problems now," Richard said.

"Best of luck, boys." Eric followed the group out of the building. He looked over at Kelly. "Now get back to your duties, lazy ass."

"I'll see them off then get right on that." Kelly followed the group.

"You'd better," Eric muttered to himself.

"Be careful out there."

"We always are," Garret said.

Kelly walked over toward the parking spaces and leaned against one of the cars. "You're not even going to tell me your plan?"

"Secrets are more fun," Skuz said. "You'll find out soon enough."

"I hate secrets."

"Get used to it," Richard said. "Now let's move out, gentlemen." He revved the deafening engine and led the group out onto the road.

Kelly looked over his shoulder back at the main building. He flung open the door and started the engine before taking off after them. He stayed a few cars behind. "Sorry, boys." He kept the procession in his sight. "We all have our jobs."

Sometime later...

"I can't believe we're actually doing this," Skuz said. "Does anyone else feel like this is surreal - what we're doing? Did we really just stop at a costume shop for a mailman outfit?"

"Don't think about it so much," Richard said.

"Ignore that," Lucien said. "You all voted for this. You need to own this."

"That's right," Garret said. "You and Irving didn't vote for this, did you?"

"Damned right, but that doesn't matter."

"It doesn't?" Skuz asked.

"No. The club has spoken. I'll support the decision, even if I disagree."

"Well said," Tony said. He looked out the window toward the unmanned motorcycles across the street. "We're only a few miles out now. How are the specifics of this going to work?"

"No bikes," Richard said. "It'd be too loud and put them on the defensive. We need them ignorant of what's happening."

Lucien's gaze moved toward the back window.

"Old man, are you listening?" Richard asked.

"Yes. Keep going."

"We're going to all go in the van. Garret gets out, drops the package, and gets back in. We leave. It's simple. Nothing can go wrong."

"Not to piss on your parade, but I think we're being followed." Lucien kept his eyes focused out the window."

"Are you sure you're not just being paranoid?" Richard asked.

"No. It's been following us since we left the Outback Boys' place. I have my guess as to who it is."

"You think Kelly followed us all the way out here to see what we were doing?" Skuz asked. "He may be curious, but I don't think even he'd do that."

"Maybe he's just watching our back," Garret suggested. "He did get us the intel after all."

"Regardless," Richard said, "it doesn't matter. Let him watch. He won't piece it together from a distance. He'll probably just end up more confused than anything."

"Yeah, you're right," Tony said. He looked down at his wrist. "It's about time for the mail to run. Now would be the time if we're going to do this."

"Alright," Richard pointed ahead out the front windshield, "then let's get this job done."

The van lurched forward down the road.

"Our guest is following." Lucien kept his gaze focused out the back.

"Keep an eye on him. Keep your weapon at the ready just in case. Don't fire until he makes a move. We don't need to cause any noise right now."

Garret encircled his arms around the package in his grasp. "God knows how much time we'd serve if we got caught with this baby in our possession."

"He's the only one who will know," Richard said. "We're getting close."

Garret rested his free hand on the car handle beside him while keeping the package steady with the other. "Stop here."

"Good luck, brother," Tony said, pulling the van to a stop in front of the designated address.

Garret slid the door open and hopped out with the box in his grip. He walked quickly up to the single-story house, dropped the box in front of their door, pushed the doorbell, and quickly made his way back to the van. He climbed inside and stared out the window.

They all watched a man open the door and look down toward his feet. He bent down and picked up the brown box before disappearing inside.

"Should we go now?" Tony asked. "I don't really want to be around when they open that thing."

"We have a bigger problem here," Lucien said. He watched a parked black van further up the road erupt with law enforcement officers flooding out of it. "Punch it!"

"What?" Tony looked in the mirror to his left and saw the incoming wall of humanity in protective armor.

"Oh, fuck me." His right foot slammed on the gas pedal.

"Looks like they had more reinforcements," Lucien said. "The men are raiding the house, and now it looks like the car branch is following us."

"This doesn't make sense." Richard's face fell forward into his hands. He mumbled through his hands. "How could they possibly know what we were doing? Never mind where we were doing it?"

"We're on a clock here. No time for reflection." Garret leaned forward between the front seats. "Tony, we need to get somewhere the eyes in the sky won't find us. I can only think of a few options for that."

"There's no decent tunnels around here. We're too far south. You're not thinking what I am, right?"

"Make for the border. They can't follow us across."

"You're serious?" Skuz asked. "We'll be walking targets down there. We don't have any connections there. Besides, what about our debt to Eric and the boys?"

"We can't pay them back if we're locked up," Garret snapped. "They'll understand."

Richard snapped out of his haze. "He's right. It looks like we're making the news tonight, boys. The only question is if we're going to be watching it from inside the pen or south of the border."

"Oh Lord above, help us." Lucien prayed, watching the flashing red and blue lights behind them. "How far are we taking this?"

"To the end."

"Weapons hot?"

"We're already resisting arrest. With the RICO act, we're fucked if we're caught. Yeah, weapons hot. Tony, you take the shortest route to the border, and drive across the barren dust if you must. Don't go to the border crossing. They'll be waiting there."

"I know the perfect off-road crossing." Tony swerved the wheel off the road. The van's cabin jerked around with every move of the wheel. The cabin bounced with every foot covered. "Provided this thing holds together."

"They're following," Lucien said.

"We're only a few minutes from the border. Keep them off my ass," Tony said, hunching forward around the steering wheel. "I don't need them ramming me right now. This is hard enough as is."

"Got it." Skuz rolled down the nearby window. "Here goes another twenty to forty years if we're caught." He leaned out the window and aimed his pistol at the following patrol cars. He squeezed off a few rounds and the leading car's windshield cracked. Red spatters of blood coated the glass. The car veered off and crashed into a tree.

"Forget the guns. Use these." Garret pulled out his special grenade. "If we place it right, it'll stop all their cars for a minute or two." He pulled Skuz away from the window, pulled the pin, and chucked it behind the van. A spectacular blue field of electricity and energy engulfed the next car, causing its engines to shut down. The car behind rear ended it and caused both to be put out of commission.

"This is getting out of hand," Lucien said. "We've got more coming in, along with a chopper above. They're gaining ground."

"Oh for God's sake. Can we not catch a break today?" Richard shouted.

"Give me your grenade." Garret jabbed his palm toward Richard. "I learned the timing. Just trust me."

Richard scrambled to place the grenade in Garret's hand. "Go for it, ace."

Garret pulled the pin, waited a few moments and tossed it above, but well below the hovering beast. The electric explosion detonated well below the helicopter. However, it did cease its forward momentum and wobbled in midair. "I think I got it."

"Good, because they're throwing the entire god damned police force at us. Now they're coming from all angles." Tony was constantly rotating the wheel, dodging police cruisers from both left and right. "We're only a minute out at this point, and they're getting desperate."

The back window exploded in a shower of glass down onto Lucien.

"Ah shit." He covered his eyes. "They're firing."

"Looks like they had enough." Richard pulled out his own weapon and fired back a few bullets behind them from out of his nearby window. "You alright, old man?"

"They got my right eye, but I'm fine." Lucien removed his hand from his head revealing a bloody right eye. He kept his eye squinted as he unholstered his own weapon and fired back. His voice raised as he fired. "You think you're going to stop me? I'll never back down, pigs!"

Skuz put a hand on Lucien's shoulder and pulled him back. "Easy, old man." He looked back at their followers. "Let me take care of this." He readied his weapon and followed his elder's example, showering the police in a hail of lead.

"Oh shit!" Tony's voice was heard just before a thundering crash along with the van lifting off the ground. The cabin tilted while in midair before crashing, causing everyone in the van to be thrown around.

A loud voice interrupted their stupor. "Exit the vehicle and keep your hands where we can see them."

The van's door was thrown open. The officer was clad

with a gas mask, Kevlar armor, and an automatic rifle. As soon as the door was open, the barrel of said rifle was pointed at everyone inside. "Don't move a muscle," his even voice warned. "Get out here." He kept the weapon pointed in their direction. He sidestepped, allowing another officer access to the cabin.

The new officer dragged the entire gang out of the van one by one, laying them out on the grass on their bellies where they were under the watchful eye of twenty armed law enforcement officers.

"Put your hands behind your heads!" One younger officer took a step toward Richard and jabbed the end of his rifle toward him.

"Easy, young man." Richard winced and moved his hands behind his head.

"Fuck you." Lucien looked up and spat on the young officer. "You took my eye, swine."

"At least we don't dabble in bioterrorism like you morons," he fired back, along with a kick to Lucien's shoulder. "Now put your hands behind your back before I do it for you."

"Go ahead." Lucien glared up at the young man. "I'd like to see you try, kid. You think I give a shit? My life's already gone."

"Hold on a minute, old man." Garret looked over beside him. "Don't lose your head."

Lucien's right hand reached up and covered his eye. "You see this? Look at it." His left hand snaked under him toward his waist. He grasped his pistol and smirked. "You see that blood pouring out?" He jumped up with the vigor of a man half his age and immediately fired a shot directly between the officer's eyes, before falling to a hail of bullets himself.

He collapsed on the soil beside Garret, his eyes wide open and unmoving.

"Son of a bitch," Garret said.

"Old man!" Skuz watched on with his hand behind his head.

"Officer down!" One of the officers cried into the radio. "We need backup and an ambulance now."

"Stubborn old coot to the last," Richard said.

"Jesus." Tony glanced down at Lucien's body as he was being escorted out of the vehicle's wreckage.

The entire gang was side by side on the ground now. "Guess we're going to be watching from the pen tonight." Richard's voice was glum and barely audible over the sirens.

"No," Garret said, "probably jail tonight. Prison will be next week"

16

"We're here," Ann said, pulling into the crowded parking lot. "Is he awake yet?" she asked, backing into the nearby parking space.

"It's been like ten minutes." Kate rubbed the side of Irving's head. "He should be waking up soon."

"Ohh." Irving sat up while cradling his head. "My head is killing me. What happened?"

"We saved your life," Ann said in a dry voice. "You just got a little too excited."

"Where are we?" Irving craned his neck to look out the car window. "Why are we at the police station?" He slowly turned back to Kate. "You're turning me in?"

"Quite the opposite actually. We saved you from being in bed with that potentially genocidal plan of your clubs?"

"What the fuck are you talking about? I never heard anything about that."

"We know. Everyone of them except Lucien and you voted for it. They blackmailed a guy at the local DDC branch to smuggle out a contagious disease to use it against

ES-15. We got you out of their clutches, told the police you'd testify, and got you out of this. Aren't you pleased?"

Irving leaned forward, cradling his head in his hands. "I...wait a minute. They were going to unleash a virus on them? What if it got loose? Oh my God. They never even asked for my vote."

"Exactly." Kate leaned against his shoulder and snuggled up next to him. "We couldn't let it potentially get out and kill thousands, could we?"

Irving went silent for a few minutes. "They're arrested already?"

"According to the radio a few minutes ago. Apparently the old man fought to his last breath," Ann said. "He shot a police officer dead before he was gunned down. That's not counting all the other damage they did on their little run toward the border."

"They were abandoning you here you know." Kate ran her hand along Irving's arm. "You would have taken all the fall if it was their choice."

"No, that's not true. It can't be."

"But it is," Ann interrupted. "Think about it. They never told you about the plan, left you behind, and tried to run out of the jurisdiction."

"Why wouldn't they at least let me know?"

"They knew you'd vote no," Kate said. "They were desperate to end this war by any means necessary. Just realize there's no other play here. If you don't testify, you're going to be in prison for the rest of your natural born life. They added a lot of charges during their little escape. Would you rather be in a prison gang, or free out here with us?"

"God dammit," Irving sighed. "That's a terrible choice,

but fine. I'll just have to hope the Outback Boys don't hunt me down. What, pray tell, did you tell them I would say?"

"You voted no on the plan, had misgivings on the whole thing, and are willing to testify against the group for complete immunity. They'll need as many witnesses as possible and should grant you that much. Remember, they're going down regardless. They were caught red handed. Be more concerned with your own prospects."

"Just what are those? Rat out my entire crew, hope I don't get hunted down by their associates, and what? Live happily ever after on the run with you two?"

"What's wrong with that?" Kate asked.

"I didn't choose this." Irving sighed. "Fine, I don't have a choice anyway at this point. Right?"

"You're taking this better than I expected," Ann said, looking toward the station.

"It's either do this, or my life's ruined. I'd much rather be with you," he grabbed Kate's hand, "especially considering I thought I'd never see you again."

"Hey, wait a minute," Ann interrupted them. She pointed toward the side of the building. A lone cruiser snuck its way around the building toward the back. "There's only one guy in there. You think that's who they delivered their package to? He looked like a cartel member."

"Why would there only be one guy?"

"Who knows?" Ann asked. "Maybe they had someone tip them off? That's never out of the realm of possibility."

"I guess you'd be the ones to know about that," Irving grumbled. "Never mind. I'm ready. Are you two staying in here or coming in with me?"

"I'm staying out here," Ann said. "I try to avoid the boys in blue when I can."

"I'll go with you. They're not actively looking for me, and I'll clear anything up that needs it."

"Shit." Irving gripped the car door handle. "I never in a million years thought I'd be testifying, but here I am. One second, the world's normal; the next, everything's upside down, with prospects of getting right side up again."

"Welcome to a life of crime. You've arrived at your destination," Ann said in a mechanical voice.

"You're a right riot," Irving said with a sharp tone. He opened the door and stepped outside. "Jesus. Why me? I'll be lucky if they don't mob me as soon as I get in the door with this on." He tugged at the leather kutte wrapped around his torso.

"You'll need that to prove my story. Don't take that off." Kate stopped him from removing it.

"If you say so." He closed the door behind her, and the pair approached the police station hand in hand. They disappeared into the building, leaving Ann to stare at the police cruisers coming and going. Her eyes wandered back to the lone cruiser. "They're not going to keep him here are they? If he's been exposed, he should go to the hospital." She watched the officers in the front get out of the car and stand around it talking. Her eyes darted back toward the front entrance. Her eyebrows raised as she saw the two come back out and enter the car. "That was fast."

"They said to come back tomorrow. They're in the middle of a dangerous transfer. Apparently the guy who got infected got away for an hour." Kate slid over and patted the seat next to her. "They know who we are though, and even offered police protection."

"Did you take it?"

"No. They'd draw more attention than us," Kate said. "We know how to be subtler than these idiots."

"Guess we're spending the next few nights in motels."

"Fantastic," Irving sarcastically mumbled.

"We'll be getting two beds, tiger. Just don't make too much noise, and I won't mind."

"Ann!" Kate reached forward and slapped Ann's shoulder. "Shut up." Her cheeks blushed a deep crimson and she looked away toward the window. "Just get us out of here."

"I am not your driver, but sure." Ann got the car moving and pulled out onto the street. "Just don't get busy yet. We don't want an indecent exposure charge to complicate things."

"Dammit, just drive." She kicked the driver's seat.

Inside the communal jail cell in the station an hour later...

Garret leaned back against the cold smooth wall. He looked to his right on the bench lining the entire wall toward Skuz and the rest of the club at his side. "We may as well get comfortable in here."

"What I want to know is how they knew." Richard's eyes narrowed and his brows furrowed. "It makes no goddamned sense."

A small wiry man stood up and scampered over toward the group. He scratched his chest and his eyes darted behind him and to the sides. "I've heard some things in here that I think you might want to know."

"Speak quickly. I'm in no mood for this," Richard growled.

"I just need a little compensation for the information. You know how this works."

"We just got here, ace," Skuz said from Richard's side.

"We haven't been to canteen yet. Do you have any idea who you're talking to?"

"You're that Order of Vengeance motorcycle group, yeah?" He twisted his neck and looked through the bars toward the desk with an officer overlooking the cell and back to the group. "Yeah, that don't mean shit here. Too many ES-15 are cooped up here. There's a huge target on all your backs in here."

"Fucking phenomenal," Garret said in a dry voice.

"Anyway, I've got connections around this place. Apparently, they've just brought in a high danger prisoner. Rumor is he's been exposed to a doomsday virus or something high powered. They're not letting anyone see him."

"It's that guy we delivered that package to no doubt," Tony said. "Have they quarantined him yet?"

"Yeah, officially."

"I don't like the sounds of this," Garret groaned.

"One of my associates in here was curious though and snuck in to see what his story was."

"Oh, shit the bed," Garret sighed. "He didn't come back into gen pop did he?"

"He did."

"We're all dead," Richard said.

"Yes. I imagine with that hit on you, you will be soon."

"No, you drooling idiot," Garret snapped. "If he got in there and back out, he just spread the contagion to the rest of the building potentially. We probably won't even get to trial, if you're telling the truth. Forget the shanks. We'll be dead in days by our own hand."

"Even me?"

"Especially you. And you probably just infected us, you jackass," Tony said, glaring at the man. "

"Anyway, he said the dude was bragging about their plan

237

working perfectly. That the dumb bikers, who I assume he was referring to you men, fell for it. He said the intel they gave you from their mole in the Outback boys played you boys like fiddles."

Richard jumped up and kicked the solid bench. "God damn Kelly. He was the one who sold us out then?"

"That's the name he said. They fed you false intel. He was bragging, trying to get rep with his new prison clique."

"It doesn't matter." Garret's head hung down. "We're all dead now because of your friend and you."

"Even if by some miracle we're not, we're getting capital punishment for our little escape plan."

"Pick your poison," Tony's glum voice said. "Shanks, virus, or lethal injection."

"I don't know about you boys, but I'd prefer to go out on my own terms," Garret said looking down to the dirty floor. "We need to find some weapons. We're already screwed. We may as well finish this war the only way we can."

"Hear, hear!" Richard said. He stood up and grabbed the short man by the scruff of his neck. "Tell us where we can find some weapons, and you'd better not hold out on us. We have nothing holding us back at this point."

"Jesus, okay. Just let me go. I know a guy in here who specializes in that kind of thing. He'll want some payment though."

"He'll be paid in not getting your and his skull smashed in," Richard said through clenched teeth.

"I'll relay the message," he wheezed out as Richard released him and pushed him away.

"You do that and make it snappy."

The man stumbled away, ran to the cell door, and started banging on it. "Hey, get me out of here!"

"It's not time for your job yet, James. Settle down."

"You should help James out, officer, for his own good of course." Richard looked over at the pair.

"Jesus, James. What did you get yourself into?" The officer opened the door and escorted him out of the cell.

"You think he'll be back?" Garret asked.

"He'll be back. He's got nowhere to hide," Tony said. "Where's he going to go? We're all in jail."

The next day...

"Great." Richard flipped the shiny new shiv in his hands. "This will work."

Garret concealed his in his pants leg. "Yeah. Now get out of here."

Tony stood watch in front of the cell. He held his hand out behind him. Garret dropped a weapon into his hand. He concealed it inside his pants, deep in his underwear. "I don't even want to imagine what you had to promise that guy to do this."

"I'll be working this off for months, or until my trial."

"Yeah, who cares?" Skuz said, inspecting his new weapon. "Just keep your trap shut, and we'll be cool."

"We have company. You should get out of here," Tony said, reaching into his pants and grabbing his shank. He pulled it out and held it at his side.

The whole club walked out of the cell into the main room and lined up, side by side. They saw the group of six ES-15 members line up opposite them.

"You're the boys our bosses were talking about, huh?" their leader asked, looking them up and down. "You don't look so tough. This will be easy."

"Easy, huh?" Garret flashed the steel in his hands. "That's what your bosses on the outside said before we kicked their asses."

"Really? From where I'm sitting, you're in the hole and he's not."

"He's sick and will be dying. Hell, your dumbass is already dead at this point. That stuff we infected him with? We're all infected in here. We're all dying. You think we give a flying fuck?" He held the shank in full view. "No."

Everyone held their weapon out pointing at their rival prison gang.

"That was you?"

"No. That was one dumbass in here going into the quarantine zone and coming back. We infected your organization from the bottom."

"That's mass murder!"

"It's not new to us." Garret sprinted forward, landed a stab to the leader's gut and pulled him into a headlock, slicing his neck open with the shank before dropping the gurgling man onto the floor.

"Oh shit!" a random prisoner yelled from his cell. "It's going down!"

"Anyone else want a shot?" Garret asked, holding his arms out wide at his sides. Skuz came up behind him and stood shoulder to shoulder, along with the rest of the club.

ES-15 followed suit, and both sides charged forward...

THANK YOU FOR READING!

I hope you enjoyed the order of vengeance story. If you'd like to support this work, please consider leaving an honest review on amazon. Have a good day!

ABOUT THE AUTHOR

Alex J Fischer has been writing for close to a decade and has won five National Novel Writing Month challenges in a row.

Alex grew up in a small town in Ohio and still resides there. Hobbies include writing, video games, and watching crime shows.

ALSO BY ALEX J. FISCHER

The Morris Crime Family Series:

Welcome To the Family

The Silver Lining

Any Means Necessary

The Fourth Bullet

A New Generation

The Order of Vengeance Motorcycle Club

Book I: The Order of Vengeance

www.ingramcontent.com/pod-product-compliance
Lightning Source LLC
Chambersburg PA
CBHW020100180626
46812CB00006B/2407